FIVE MINUTE STORIES

VOLUMES ONE - FIVE

By Jennifer Brozek

"A little bit of story to last you all day."

Five Minute Stories

Volumes One – Five

3/2018

Jennifer Brozek

Apocalypse Ink Productions
Kenmore, Washington

Credits

Five Minute Stories, Volume 1 ©2017 Jennifer Brozek
Five Minute Stories, Volume 2 ©2017 Jennifer Brozek
Five Minute Stories, Volume 3 ©2017 Jennifer Brozek
Five Minute Stories, Volume 4 ©2017 Jennifer Brozek
Five Minute Stories, Volume 5 ©2017 Jennifer Brozek

Portions of this book were previously published in *In a Gilded Light* ©2010 Jennifer Brozek

All rights reserved. No part of the contents of this book may be reproduced or transmitted in any form or by any means without the written permission of Apocalypse Ink Productions.

Interior design by Jeff Brozek

PUBLISHED BY
Apocalypse Ink Productions
6830 NE Bothell Way, STE C #404
Kenmore, WA 98028
http://www.apocalypse-ink.com/

First Published June 2017
Second Edition October 2017

This is a work of fiction. All characters and events portrayed in this novel are either products of the author's imagination or are used fictitiously.

ISBN: 978-1-940444-26-0

*These are the things I think about all day.
I hope you enjoy a peek into my brain.*

~Jennifer Brozek

Table of Contents

- Volume One 1
  - Number 42 3
  - Camouflage 7
  - Nifty Gifty 10
  - Good Friday Sacrifice 13
  - Aversion Therapy 16
  - Watch Me 19
  - Parkour Hacking 22
  - Young Love 25
  - Anchors 28
  - How the Monster Really Works 30
  - The VIP Treatment 33
  - The Harpsichord 37
  - Red and White and Bad for Your Heart 41
- Volume Two 43
  - Finishing Touches 45
  - A Grave Mistake 48
  - Questions 51
  - Overheard 54
  - Listen to Me 56
  - Happy 59
  - Not So Crystal Ball 62
  - Train to Topeka 64
  - The Last Present 67
  - Phobias 70
  - What a Real Psychic Would Do 73
  - Shadowplay 76
  - Room Service 80
- Volume Three 83
  - Bedside Manner 85
  - Happy Anniversary 87
  - Good-Bye 90
  - Nightmare Revelation 92
  - Considered a Success 96
  - Artist Interrupted 98
  - The Perfect Match 101

- Ice Pops 104
- Addictions 108
- Undressing & Dressing 110
- The Pact 114
- Rivalry.. 117
- Dust Bunnies 120
- Volume Four... 125
  - Diamonds Are Forever 127
  - Collateral Damage 131
  - Locks of Love... 134
  - Interloper 137
  - The EMP Touch 140
  - Following Advice 144
  - Hell is Other People 146
  - Ink 150
  - A Special Breed.. 153
  - No Names... 156
  - Love Bites... 158
  - Directions... 161
  - We Don't Open Random Doors in this House... 164
- Volume Five.. 167
  - Responsible 169
  - The Perfect Cut for the Perfect Match 172
  - Voicemail.. 175
  - Two Letters 178
  - Waiting.. 181
  - A Gentleman's Protection 184
  - One Big Lie 187
  - Within the Lines 191
  - Origin Story? 194
  - The New Line 196
  - Cassandra's Little Brother 200
  - Legacy 203
  - Elevator of the Damned 206
- About the Author... 210

Five Minute Stories

Volume One

Number 42

WHEN BRETT WOKE, it was because of the silence. It shouldn't be silent on a Greyhound bus. Even if they were stopped for gas or a break to stretch the legs, it wouldn't be silent. There would be sounds of traffic and people and general life. Instead, there was nothing. His own breathing was loud in his ears. His heart felt like it would pound out of his chest.

Something was very wrong.

He sat up and peeked around the seat in front of him. He wasn't in the last seat on the bus but almost. Looking up the aisle, he saw nothing but empty seats in the gray twilight. It disturbed him that he couldn't tell if it was a morning twilight or an evening one. He wanted to know if the sun was rising or if he would soon be in total darkness. Looking out the window to his left, the sky was no help. The uniform gray of the clouds told him nothing of the time.

Brett stood then crouched again. Standing allowed him to see out the right side of the bus. He was in great danger. He had seen a row of bodies lined up side-by-side... and something moving. Still crouched, he duck-walked his way up to the front of the bus. The door was open and freezing cold air streamed into the Greyhound's still warm interior. Whatever happened had just happened.

He got as close to the door as possible without revealing himself and listened. The thing moving out there was a person; a man. He was counting to himself. "39, 40, 41.... There should be 42. How am I missing one? There should be 42 bodies. I don't lose people. No one gets away from me." The man started counting the bodies again, beginning with the bodies farthest from the door.

Moving as quickly and as quietly as he could, Brett eased from the bus and slipped around to the front, keeping the bus between him and the insane man who had somehow killed all his fellow travelers. Brett looked forward and saw nothing but an empty stretch of road covered in snow. They were no longer on the main interstate. Instead, they were on a smaller highway. Sneaking to the other side of the bus, he was dismayed that the road back looked almost as featureless as the road ahead—except for a road sign he couldn't read from the back.

Without warning, the bus rocked. The Counting Man had gotten on it, looking for his missing body number 42. Brett knew he wouldn't be happy to find his last victim still alive and wouldn't hesitate to remedy the situation. Sticking close to the side of the bus, he watched the man's darkened form travel the length of the vehicle.

Sensing something, the Counting Man suddenly turned and pressed his face to the window. He and Brett locked eyes. Brett realized that the man wore a Greyhound driver's uniform and was furious. The man saw Brett, saw him living and breathing, and yelled. Brett didn't hear what was yelled, but he didn't hesitate. He sprinted off down the road towards the road sign. At worst, it would tell him where he was. At best, he would be able to outrun his pursuer and wouldn't become body number 42.

Quicker than he thought possible, the driver was on his heels, shouting at him, "Wait up! You've got a special destination, boy. Wait up!"

Looking over his shoulder, he saw the driver reaching for him. Behind the driver was the I-94 W sign. It was still the interstate, but not any stretch of it he recognized. That meant they were either leaving Minnesota or entering North Dakota. That meant civilization. He did what any other person would do at this point. He put on a burst of speed born of fear, but it was no use. A hand landed on his shoulder, "Wait up, boy!"

"No!" He whirled and struck out at the man who mercifully let go.

"Whoa, boy! Wake up. Wake up! It's a nightmare."

Blinking in confusion, but fully alert, Brett found himself back on the bus and one of his fellow travelers, a Southern man—*Number 39*, he thought—backed away from him. "What? Where am I?"

"Greyhound bus from Portland, Maine to Portland, Oregon. You were having a nightmare. Twitching and moaning. Just wanted to wake you. Let you know we've stopped for a break and a change of driver."

Brett sat up. "Where are we? Where?"

"I-94 West, near Swan Lake. You all right?

"Yeah. I am now." He stood and walked to the front of the bus, changed his mind and came back, passing Number 39 on the way. The man grunted amicably at him as he passed. Brett gathered up his meager belongings: a backpack and a shoulder bag. He needed to have his things with him.

He was stopped at the exit from the bus by the two drivers standing there. Both men were familiar. One was the one from Portland, Maine.

The other was from his dream. For a long moment, Brett couldn't move, speak, or even breathe. Finally, the two drivers turned to look at him.

"Something wrong?" the first one asked.

"Going somewhere?" the second one asked.

"Yes." He said with a small explosion of breath as an answer to both questions.

"Wait a second," said the driver from his dream. "Who are you? I don't lose any of my passengers on these trips. No one gets forgotten."

"I'm number 42 and you've just lost me." Brett pushed past the two men. One of them looked confused. The other looked angry.

He didn't stop to turn around. It was all coming back to him now. He had been on the run for a long time, living by his wits alone. They had been out to get him for forever it seemed. They had almost gotten him this time. Almost.

Camouflage

WENDY SIGHED AT the latest email in her inbox. There was only so much stress a person could take. It was time for a walk. She put on her headphones and headed out of the building, taking one of the many forested trails that wound its way behind and between the buildings on the Microsoft campus. This particular trail ran uphill past Building 36. The way she was feeling, she would find out what the trail was like that far up. While her music played, she stomped along, enjoying the clomping sound her feet made against the little wooden bridge. The normally persistent ducks, that begged for food from everyone, shied away from her in a flurry of feathers and discontented quacks.

Wendy felt guilty for scaring the ducks and that it had made her smile. She shouldn't take her annoyance at her co-workers out on the hapless beings—especially ducks. With an effort, she swallowed her anger and let it drain out her feet with every step. A couple of songs later, she was feeling much better.

She realized that she was coming up on Building 36. She saw its familiar shored up garage wall of rock and wire. In no mood to turn around, Wendy kept on going. She slowed to enjoy the unfamiliar twists and turns, looking all around, noting where, through the underbrush, she could see the former road cut into the banks on either side of her. She tried to remember which buildings were on the other side of Building 36 and if she would have to cut across a parking lot to keep going.

She was deep enough inside her mind that the thing swaying about fifteen feet from her at head height kicked in the hindbrain's reptilian response and startled her. There was a moment of frozen fight-or-flight hesitation before Wendy's rational brain took over and identified the thing: a half-inflated Mylar balloon with a cartoon ogre face on it.

She laughed at her jumpiness and kept going, chiding herself for being so tense. It was clear she needed this walk more than she had realized. Continuing on, she huffed and puffed up a steep part of the trail, realizing just how out of shape she was. Yes, part of her problem was not enough exercise. Exercise helped deal with stress and it was clear she wasn't dealing with it well right now.

Coming around the bend at the top of the steepest part of the trail, a second Mylar balloon startled her again, but not as much as it had the first time. This one was about ten feet from the trail to the right, swaying in the wind at people head height. She shook her head and wondered if one of the teams here had had a "Shrek" themed product release party or something like that.

Now, she looked for the shiny partly inflated balloons, expecting them. She didn't want to be startled again. Along with being somewhat out of shape, she knew she was borderline hypertensive and she didn't need to give herself a heart attack. Her mind started rambling off in that direction when there was movement behind her. Still more keyed up than she wanted to admit, Wendy whipped around and stared. She also listened intently until she realized that she still had her headphones on and all she could hear was her music.

Wendy took off the headphones and wrapped them around her mp3 player. She stared for a long time in the direction she was certain the movement came from; listening and looking. She knew the movement came from where the other Mylar balloon had been. But, all she could hear and see were the birds and bugs. Nothing more. Again, shaking her head, she had to wonder at her own sanity. She turned back in the direction she had been going and dropped her mp3 player.

Less than five feet away on the left side of the trail was another balloon just like the other two she had just seen. It couldn't be the same one. That was impossible. This one seemed stuck to a squat tree. She couldn't figure out how she missed it. Was it because she had been concentrating on what seemed to be going on behind her?

Wendy stepped up to the tree and reached out for the balloon, but it swayed to the side. For the first instant, she thought it had been covering an ugly carving in the trunk of the tree. In the second, she knew the face in the tree was alive and it was not a tree at all. She took a breath and turned with the intention of screaming and running for her life. She never got the chance.

Its arm shot out and grabbed her by the face, halting her motion and muffling her scream. It yanked her forward into its arms as it swung her into the underbrush at the side of the trail. She was unable to utter a sound as the thing... the ogre... brought her to the ground and ripped out her throat with yellowed fangs while the Mylar balloon tied to its wrist bobbed merrily over them, watching its owner's feeding frenzy with silent shininess.

Nifty Gifty

MONTE SENT OFF the last of the *Nifty Gifty* emails to those who wanted to participate in the Halloween gift swap. He marveled at how easily people would hand over personal information they normally considered sacred when they thought they were going to get something free out of it. Each person from the online community participating in the *Nifty Gifty* gift swap was assigned a partner and a scavenger list of things that person wanted. It would be a lot of fun for everyone. Himself included. Everyone knew who their swap partner was. It wasn't the 'secret Santa' kind of round-robin gift giving that he preferred.

That would come later.

He figured he would do the real gift-giving in January when the holiday gift giving was over and no one would be expecting anything. That was when he would set up the real round robin gift giving and when the survey he had everyone fill out would come in handy. There was one particular question he was most interested in: What is your favorite part of the body?

After he placed the eleven names into the bag, he started pulling them out one by one and making a note on each of their cards:

Alex – hands
Ryan – legs
Sara – eyes
Christina – brain
Rick – legs
Gynn – hands
Joe – butt
Bill – breasts
Monica – hair
Amy – feet

Monte smirked at his list. Perfect. There would be enough to go around. He couldn't have asked for a better spread.

The last name he pulled from the hat was "Johanna." She was the luckiest of the bunch. This was good. He was already friends with her. He had her address. The rest would be simple. He knew her kinks. Given her proclivities, getting her in a compromising position that involved bondage would be a piece of cake.

At that point, he could transport her to a private place of his choosing and make the special surprise gifts from her. She would be famous by the end of the next month. That would be his gift to her.

Next, he made up the package labels he would eventually use. Ryan's gift would come from Alex; Sara's from Ryan; Christina's from Sara and so on until the list wrapped around and Alex's gift would come from Amy. Monte paused and thought about Alex's gift. Alex had a thing for hands. It was *too* perfect. That disturbed him.

For a brief moment, he wondered if his online friends were on to his true gift giving plans. That they'd gotten together and discussed it, spreading out the body parts amongst them. That they wanted these gifts and were expecting them.

No. They couldn't be. That was just crazy talk. He had randomly drawn Alex's wife, Johanna, last. There was no way for Alex to know just how well it suited this little game Monte had planned.

No. These gifts would be a real surprise.

There was a glimmer in Monte's eyes and he let loose a sharp, barking laugh that only close friends would recognize as a sign of pleasure at an idea he had just had. Of course, this new idea would mean that he would have to learn taxidermy, bone cleaning and body preservation. Most of the gifts could be stripped clean to the bone but the body parts like breasts and butt would have to be preserved and stuffed. The scalp of her hair would have to be tanned. Yet another thing he needed to learn. Then again, learning was the spice of life.

Originally, he had planned to send these body part gifts as fresh as possible, packed in dry ice, but he couldn't get the idea of a cleaned, bony hand wearing its wedding ring gripping a scroll with the words, *'Until death do we part...'* written on it in ornate calligraphy, out of his head. He could already imagine the look on Alex's face as he realized exactly what the gift was.

That would be a real nifty gifty!

Good Friday Sacrifice

"**TODAY IS MY** day. It's my birthday. My own personal Good Friday." Lynn waded through the forest underbrush.

"I'm sorry." Cherie looked away.

"Sorry? Why?" Lynn paused by a tree.

"It's Friday the 13th. It's unlucky."

"No. It's not. Not for most people."

"Yes, it is. My mom says so..."

"Your mom also believes that science fiction books are a satanic plot designed to make people more accepting of the Antichrist when he shows up in a flying saucer." Lynn shrugged, before continuing their trek.

Cherie grimaced then followed. "Yeah. I know. Mom's an odd duck, but I've never had a 'good' Friday the 13th. Ever."

"I was born on a Friday the 13th. It's what makes me special. Did you know every year has at least one Friday the 13th? Or as many as three? The 13th is more likely to fall on a Friday than any other day of the week because of Leap Year rules. Special things happen on Friday the 13th."

"I didn't know that." She was silent for a long time. "What is so special about Friday the 13th for you?"

"All Friday the 13ths are good days, but when it lands on my birthday, it's special. Then, it's *my* day. It's when they first came to me. I was six. They gave me this locket." She gestured to the plain silver locket she wore. "I use it to call them to me if I need to.

"The next time I saw them I was eleven, and old enough to understand what they were, that they were there to protect me; that I was their focus in this world to keep it safe from all outside things.

But, they needed something back, the sacrifice of something important to me and they needed it on my birthday when the dates aligned. It was the price of being special in this world. That day, I thought about what to give them. I decided on the thing I loved most: my kitten, Whiskers."

The two of them stopped in the middle of an opening in the forest. It was too small to be called a glade. Cherie frowned. "I don't understand. What'd they do with Whiskers? I thought you said that coyotes got him. *They* who anyway?"

"You'll know soon enough."

Lynn reached out a hand and pushed Cherie to the side. She took two off-balance steps and fell as the grass gave way beneath her. She landed hard on her right shoulder and hip. At first, the pain was too sharp to move. When she could move, she rolled to her back and saw Lynn kneeling at the top of a fifteen foot drop.

"I'm sorry, Cherie. I thought about skimping this time; to give them my dog or even my little brother. But, in my deepest of hearts, I do love you best and that's why I have to sacrifice you. I promised never to be false to them or to my duty to this world."

Cherie got to her feet, feeling every bruise. "What are you talking about? Help me out of here."

"I can't. I wish I could. I can't. If I did, they wouldn't take care of me or anyone anymore." Lynn was crying now.

"I don't understand. You're really scaring me." She put out her arms to make sure she didn't bump into anything.

"They've always been there for me. Remember when I fell out of the tree when I was nine? I should have been paralyzed. I wasn't because they caught me. Remember the car accident two years ago? We should've been killed? We weren't because they were there and changed things just enough. There are a lot of other things they've done to help me and to protect the rest of the world. I would tell you, but there's no time."

"Lynn, accidents happen and people survive them every day. Just-just like this accident. Help me out of here. Please!" Cherie tried to keep the fear from her voice, but she thought she could hear sounds in the dark around her; sounds of inhuman things moving towards her. "Please!" She made her way to the wall of the hole and felt nothing but soft earth. There was nothing to hold onto; nothing to climb.

"I'm sorry. It's my duty and my curse. I'm really going to miss you. I'm so sorry."

As Lynn spoke her last apology to her best friend, she covered the hole with the grass sod. It was harder this time. Harder than she thought possible to turn away from that silence in the hole. Cherie didn't scream. Lynn would know when the sacrifice of her most beloved was taken. They would tell her and all would be safe in the world until the next time.

The next Good Friday Sacrifice would be in 2017. She would be twenty-six. She hoped to God she wasn't married and wouldn't have to sacrifice her husband or one of her own children. But, she was special and she would do what she had to do to keep this world safe.

Aversion Therapy

"**Are you sure** about this, Doctor?" Sara was nervous, but still determined to overcome her irrational fear.

Dr. Stewart nodded. "I am. You did the research. You read the paperwork. You know what your problem is. You know I don't take on patients I don't believe I can help. After studying your problem, I took on your case because I *knew* I could help you. That this type of therapy is the best thing you can do with your particular issue."

"It's because of my childhood ear infections. Any water in my ears would cause horrible, painful ear infections." She repeated this for the hundredth time. "I can't go swimming because of it. I can't even dunk my head underwater in the bathtub because of the memory of them."

"Then there are the dreams."

Sara stared at her feet. "Yeah. Dreams of being drowned by someone."

Dr. Stewart nodded. "Yes. We'll deal with all of that. Are you ready?"

She looked at the large glass tank before her. It looked like the kind of tank a magician used in a death-defying underwater escape trick. She shuddered at the thought of what she was about to do. Then, she steeled herself. "Yes. I'm ready," she said and started towards the ladder.

"Wait." Dr. Stewart's command froze her with one hand reaching for the ladder. "I have a gift for you." He handed her a pair of earplugs. "Just in case. I would hate for you to get another ear inflection because of me. I want you to be as comfortable as possible before and after."

Sara took the earplugs without comment and offered him a weak smile as she put the earplugs in.

"Aversion therapy isn't pleasant, but I promise you'll never be bothered by those dreams again." He gave her shoulder a reassuring squeeze and stepped back.

She climbed the ladder and dropped herself into the tank. He let her get comfortable with her surroundings and waited until she nodded to him to turn the water on. Once he did, the water rushed in a torrent of water at her feet. The doctor returned to the camcorder, turning it on and focusing it on the tank.

"This is high enough, Doc," Sara called when the water was at her waist.

He shook his head. "You need to get your head wet." He smiled as he watched her discomfort at the swiftly rising water.

"No. Really. This is high enough, Dr. Stewart." Sara hit the thick glass when the water reached her breast line. "I can dunk my head now."

Again, Dr. Stewart shook his head. "No. I'm sorry. Remember, you're not the one in control." Then, he seemed to remember something and walked over to the tank. "One last thing."

"I can't do this! I can't do it! Stop the water!" Sara's voice was high and sharp with fear. The water level was at her collarbone now.

He touched a control on the back of the tank and the lid clanged shut and locked in place with the loud clack of a bolt turning. Dr. Stewart walked back to the camcorder while Sara screamed at him to let her out. The water lapped over her nose and mouth. In less than a minute, it would be over her head. He watched through the camcorder as Sara pounded against the lid of the tank.

"Aren't you supposed to drain the water now?" Mrs. Stewart asked, coming in from behind her husband.

"Only if that was her real fear. Her real fear was the nightmare of being drowned by someone. I am curing her of that right now. No man killed her. She killed herself." He watched Sara with great interest as she slapped at the glass wall with failing strength. "She agreed to everything and signed all the paperwork. Another cured patient. Also, this gives you another flower for your bone garden."

Mrs. Stewart fluttered her eyelashes at him. "You're so sweet to me." She leaned forward, kissed him on the cheek and then stood in silence as the two of them watched until the final bubbles of air drifted from Sara's floating body.

Watch Me

"**Is that David's** watch?" Joe asked.

Lynn nodded. "He left it behind when he... you know."

"Left you in a lurch? Yeah. I know. That's my little bro. Always the slacker. Never someone who cared about things that matter."

"Not like you." Her voice was flat.

"Not like me." Joe agreed as he pulled her to him. "C'mere babe. Lemme show you how much I appreciate you."

Lynn ducked the kiss and half-smiled. "You did that last night." She held out the watch. "Try it on?"

He frowned. "It's David's."

"David's gone. I know you've always admired it. I think you should have it. I want to show you my appreciation of you." She gestured with it. "You deserve it. He left me alone and you came to take care of me. He did exactly what you've always told me he'd do."

Joe took the watch and admired it in the light. "Yeah. I do deserve it. Dad shouldn't have given it to him. It should've been mine by right. I'm the oldest." He snapped it around his wrist.

"It's a little tight like I thought it might be."

"It's fine. I'm just big boned."

"You know what?" She smiled a genuine smile, reached for his wrist, and unsnapped the too tight watchband. "I'm going to get some links added to the watch. You deserve every bit of what's coming to you."

Something in the tone of her voice made him draw back from her. But, by then, it was too late. Joe blurred and faded before her eyes. Even as he reached for her, panicked, he disappeared as his hand passed through her. Blurring and reappearing in his place was David.

David gasped, startled. He reached out, grabbing her to him. "I thought I'd never see you again!"

She held onto him for dear life. "I never gave up on you. I'm so sorry I took the watch from you. I didn't know what it was. I was just.... Are you all right?"

He shuddered against her. "I am now. How long was I gone? It felt like forever."

"Only two weeks."

"Two weeks? It felt like years. I was there, seeing things happening to you and my family, but I couldn't do anything about it and it was all out of order. Is my Dad okay?"

She nodded. "He's shaken and still a little shell shocked. Doctors think he had a psychotic episode. That's their theory on why he's been missing all these months. They don't believe anything about him being lost in time."

"You saved me." He looked her in the face and smiled. "I love you." Then, he frowned. "Who's... gone now?"

"Joe."

"My brother? Damn. I wouldn't wish that on him even though he *is* my worst enemy."

She scowled. "He deserved it."

He saw the look on her face and gave her a worried frown. "What happened?"

Lynn shook her head. "Doesn't matter. What matters is that we have to destroy this thing. I don't want anyone else getting snagged and I sure as hell don't want Joe coming back." She gestured the watch at him. "I'm gonna take it apart until there is nothing left but gears and springs. Then I'm going to break those, too."

"I think that'll kill him."

"I don't care. Joe's been a rat bastard from day one."

"Could you really do that? To anyone?"

"To Joe? Watch me."

David watched in silence as Lynn took a small set of screwdrivers to the ordinary looking watch. She took it apart bit by bit. As she removed each new piece, she paused to mangle it in some way. Finally, all that was left was the watch crystal.

"I think it's working. The scar from where my brother pushed me out of the tree is gone."

She held up the watch crystal to her eye. "What was that, hon?"

"I was asking if you wanted to go see Dad in the hospital. The doctors think it will help him."

"Sure. I'm glad he's back." She tilted her head. "Huh, that's funny. I swear I see an image of someone who looks almost like you in this."

"That's because you're looking through it at me." He gestured to the watch remains. "Face it, Lynn, you're never going to fix that old watch."

She sighed. "I know. I was hoping it would help get your dad's memory back. It's nothing but trash now."

Scooping the watch remains into the wastebasket she gave the unbroken watch crystal a last look and shook her head. It really did look sort of like a ghostly image of David's face was frozen in a scream in the glass. It was some trick of the light she thought before tossing it into the trash with the rest of the broken pieces.

Parkour Hacking

"**Lemme get this** straight. It's a combination of the parkour and computer hacking?" Ted asked, his eyebrows furrowed.

"Yep. The ultimate balance in mind and body. Kind of like that new sport, chess-boxing. But, instead of a round of boxing followed by a round of chess, you have to get from point A to point B and the obstacles include hacking a computer system or three to continue on." Mark grinned. "I used to be the world champion. Now, I'm retired, rich, and recruiting."

Ted considered his new friend. The man was certainly rich, in good shape, and had been able to hold his own at DefCon. "How come I've never heard of it?"

"Because it's pretty much illegal. What city's gonna want a bunch of hyped up Traceurs racing across their rooftops, pelting down their streets and hacking into locked buildings all in the name of fun and a six digit prize?"

"Point conceded. What happens if we do get caught and arrested wherever this parkour hacking event is being held?"

"We bail you out and buy off whoever needs to be bought." Mark lit a cigarillo and puffed on it. "It's all part of your entry fee."

"Speaking of that, how much is the entry fee?"

"$500 per race."

Ted's smile collapsed. "You've got to be shitting me."

"Nope... but the payout is $500,000 per race for the winner." Mark grinned at the dollar signs in Ted's eyes. "I don't recruit just anyone. They have to be the best—smart and fast in both brain and brawn. That, my friend, is you."

"What do you get out of it?"

"Isn't it obvious?"

"Just tell me."

"I bet on you against other recruiters and players. The money that I toss around on these events makes your pay out look like chump change."

"When do I gotta tell you yea or nay?"

"Now. If you say 'no' I'm off to my next recruitment subject."

"If I say yes?"

"I call your entry in. We walk you to your bank for the cash and off we go."

"Just like that?"

"Just like that."

"Who's your next recruitment guy?"

Mark puffed on his cigarillo. "Huh. No one's asked me that before. I really shouldn't tell you." He shrugged. "Doug Littleton."

"You're kidding."

"Nope."

"He couldn't hack his way out of a paper bag. He's all right at parkour, but not computers."

Mark shrugged. "You take what you can get. Are you in or out?"

Ted considered it for about a full minute before he nodded. "I'm in."

"Great. Go give whomever you need to a call that you're gonna be gone for a couple of days. I'm gonna call your entry in."

Ted nodded and walked off, pulling out his cell phone.

Mark pulled out his own cell phone. "I got you another one. Ted Underman. Yeah. I know. I'm good. What can I say? They always think it's legit when you tell them first, that it is illegal and second, that they have to pay to play."

He listened and nodded. "I think we should put Underman as one of the hunters and the Littleton kid as one of the hunted. ...Yeah. The Littleton kid's slow on the hacking. He should be one of the first to die in a spectacular manner. It'll boost the ratings. If Underman won't hunt, we'll have no choice but to make him one of the hunted. But, you know, when they know the real score—kill or be killed—they always go for hunter."

Mark looked up. "He's coming back. See you tonight." He pocketed his phone. "We all set?"

Ted nodded. "Yeah. I don't suppose you take a check."

"Nope."

"Didn't think so. Let's hit the bank." Ted grinned at his new manager.

The manager grinned back at his newest victim. "Let's do it. You ready to start a new life of adrenaline and excitement?"

"Hell yeah!"

"That's the spirit. I knew I could count on you."

Young Love

"**How does that** feel?" Isabel asked Laura as she adjusted the heated and scented rolled towel beneath Laura's neck.

"It feels wonderful. Thank you."

"And you, sir?" Patrick asked Devon.

"I'm good. Thanks." Devon said.

Both Laura and Devon had been well massaged with fragrant oils and were sleepy with pleasure at the expert practices of the spa attendants. They smiled at each other, winking and mouthing the words, "I love you" across the small room.

"Now, while the oils soak into your skin under the heated towels, we're going to hook you two up to the oxygen therapy masks. Both scented in vanilla and lavender as requested. Remember, as you breathe in the almost pure oxygen, you may feel lightheaded or a little dizzy. That will pass." Isabel told the happy couple as Patrick brought out the oxygen masks.

Devon reached out a hand to Laura who reached out and clasped his. They squeezed each other's hands until the oxygen masks were adjusted over their respective faces. Then the two spa attendants replaced the messed up towels after Devon and Laura retrieved their arms and settled in for their skin softening soak.

"We'll be back in about fifteen minutes. Feel free to completely relax. Many of our clients fall asleep at this point. We'll wake you for the next part of it." Patrick and Isabel left the dim, warm spa room not expecting and not receiving an answer. They stood outside, watching the couple through the small window and waited.

"She's pretty." Isabel gestured to the window.

"Not as pretty as you when I first laid eyes upon you."

She turned to him. "I, of course, hated you on sight."

Patrick gave her a gentle kiss. "Of course you did, it was your duty as the captive princess of a conquered king." He looked into the past. "I remember how you fought me until you discovered that not only was I not such an awful man; I'd learned the secret to immortality... that it could only be attained and shared while in love."

The two of them continued to watch the young lovers through the window in the door. "Ah," Patrick said as he saw Devon's arm slide limply from the massage table. "There he goes."

"Do you ever miss the fighting and struggles? The screams of terror until we made it so they wouldn't or couldn't scream anymore?" Isabel asked with a nostalgic smile.

He thought about it. "No. Not really. Too messy."

She sighed. "I do. Sometimes. It always got my blood up. Mad hot and horny."

"Oh, yes? He's already gone. Should I wake her up and tell her what's going to happen to her and her new husband?"

"No. Too late. Look, she's gone, too. Head lulled. Her other arm's just flopped off the table. Brain dead and helpless. No struggles there." Isabel sighed again.

They opened the doors and walked in. They went to the unconscious couple and removed them from their heavy, heated towels. She took a deep breath. "What did you use on him?"

"Oil olive."

"Of course. No, the spices."

"Rosemary, thyme, and tarragon."

"Oh, that should taste divine!"

"What about her?" He asked as he came over and helped shift Laura's limp, naked body to the rolling metal table.

"Olive oil, basil, pepper and, of course, Kosher salt. Not that she's Kosher or anything."

"Sounds wonderful."

Isabel turned to him. "I think we should tell the cooks that these two should be roasted with their hands clasped. Kind of like what they did just before we left the room. It was so romantic. If we're going to eat the flesh and hearts of young lovers to stay young forever, I want the presentation to be just as romantic."

"That's why I love you so much." The two of them lifted Devon's limp, naked body to the rolling metal table.

"Why?" She gave him a coy smile.

"One moment, you're nostalgic about doing things the old vicious and brutal way. The next, you're being all sweet and sappy. You're so complex. You always keep me guessing."

"Thank you, dearest of my heart. I try. What's the use of youth and beauty if every day is the same?"

"True. We'll make sure the cooks roast them with their hands clasped. It will make for a magnificent feast. How many other couples made it to this year's meal?"

"Just four. There'll be plenty of young love and beauty to go around. And we know they'll taste wonderful with their flesh oiled to perfection."

Anchors

THE RINGING PHONE distracted Bob from his conversation. He looked at the cell phone's caller ID and answered when he saw that it was Emma. "Ciao-ciao."

"Heya, Bob. It's Emma."

"Long time."

"I know. I'm sorry. I've been under a rock—or more like a writing tablet—getting this book done."

"You finished?"

"Yeah. I'm really tired and really happy."

"Congrats, dear. I'm happy for you."

There was a pause. "I didn't call because of the book."

"No?"

"No. I called because I just wanted to tell you I love you. That I've always loved you and I wanted you to know it."

He frowned, "What brought this on?"

"You heard about the real bad storms we've been having out here, right?"

"Yeah."

"Well, we lost power and I ran out of cell phone charge and I started thinking and wondering what if this was it? What if we never got our power back? What would I lose? I realized how much my life was tied up with people from far away.

"One of the things that would devastate me the most would be losing you. I know we talk about how I'm an anchor for you in your life and have been since college, but I realized right then and there how much you've been an anchor for me, too. I really wanted to tell you that and to say I love you and to let you know. I was kinda afraid I wouldn't get the chance. You know?"

"I'm an anchor for you?"

"Yeah. I know it sounds... weird. Me being me and all."

"No. It doesn't. Thank you for telling me. And, Emma?"

"Yeah?"

"I love you, too."

"Thanks, bro."

There was another long pause then Emma coughed. "I hate to dump all of this emotional squee on you and run, but I gotta go. Talk to you in a couple of weeks?"

"Yeah. I'll talk to you then."

"Bye."

"Ciao-ciao."

Bob hung up the phone, put it back down on the table, and looked at it for a long time. Then, he un-cocked the .45 caliber pistol in his right hand and put it on the table next to the phone. "I guess you and I will have to finish our conversation sometime later." He spoke to the weapon in a soft, contemplative voice. "It looks like someone still needs me for me. It's not my time to rest."

He got up from the table and walked to the closet where he kept his gun cleaning kit. He mused that he suddenly knew what would keep a man going when duty was no longer enough. It was an epiphany worth remembering.

How the Monster Really Works

JULIE HATED BEING the third wheel. But, there she was, bumping along after the couple in front of her as they walked down to the river. Kirsti was her best friend. Kai was the boy they'd both loved since grade school. Once, they were an inseparable threesome. Now, not so much.

They arrived at the river at sunset. "Isn't this gorgeous?" Kirsti asked.

"Yes." Kai looked at Kirsti instead of the view. Kirsti blushed and hugged him tight.

Behind them Julie rolled her eyes. Her two best friends had started dating a few weeks ago, cutting her out of their rapport. Their threesome had become a couple and a third wheel. It'd hurt her more than she was willing to admit.

The river used to be their favorite spot. She had suggested an evening picnic to see if they could recapture the connection they'd once had. She needed to see if they could be a threesome again; if they would include her.

Julie had been patient. She'd waited over two hours, well after sunset, before she had to admit it was a lost cause. Kirsti and Kai were curled up together on the log before the fire, murmuring to each other, punctuating their thoughts with kisses. Oh, sure, there had been an attempt at including Julie. Several, even. During dinner. During a game of flashlight Frisbee. During storytelling. But, each time, it'd devolved into Kirsti and Kai with Julie on the outside again. Each knowing look, each secret smile, and each sweet kiss was slap in the face. Their threesome was gone and it was time to walk away.

"Oh, damn. My flashlight's going out. I should go get some more batteries." She stood with an abrupt jerk. "I'll be back soon."

"Okay." Kai said.

"Be careful, Okay?" Kirsti added.

"I will." Julie headed back down the wooden path, listening to the rest of her friends' conversation.

"Shouldn't we go with her?"

"Nah." Kai's voice floated to her. "She'll be fine. Besides, if a monster comes, she'll be eaten first to show the audience how the monster works. That's what you get for going off alone."

"Kai! That's awful!"

She heard the two of them laugh. Yes. It was awful. Julie knew Kai would feel horrible if she did die on the way back to the house. It would serve him right, making such a mean crack like that. He'd feel guilty for the rest of his life. So would Kirsti. However, she would be dead and that would be no fun. Julie wouldn't get to enjoy their pain and that was no good. She walked along for a while, pondering the thought of revenge and the fact that revenge wasn't worth it if you couldn't savor the results.

A branch breaking to her right caught her attention. There was a rustle of leaves and branches in a clear sign that something was there. She stepped away from the tree line by the path and waved her flashlight at the brush. Something big moved through the foliage to stay out of the light. It circled her and she couldn't tell where it was. Julie turned around and around, frantically turning the beam of light this way and that. "Who's there?"

She whirled again and turned the beam full on the creature. It was huge and furry with claws and a mouth filled with fangs. For a moment, neither of them moved. Then the monster snapped out a clawed paw and grabbed the wrist of the hand holding the flashlight. Julie yelped and slapped at the monster's paw.

Stung, the monster snatched his paw back and cowered from her.

"Oh, no. I'm sorry, baby. I didn't mean to do that. You startled me." Julie cooed, reaching out gently to pet the monster's arm. "I know you don't like the light, but I need it to see."

The monster stopped cringing and whined at her.

"I'm sorry. Are you all right? Are you hungry?"

It nodded its huge, shaggy head.

"Good. Because I got you two this time. Just down by the river. A guy and a girl. But, remember, you've got to kill one immediately. Then, you can eat the other one slowly. Understand?"

The monster nodded and trilled a question at her.

"No. I don't care which one. Just enjoy." Julie petted the monster some more. "Don't I always take care of you?"

It nodded again and hugged her.

"All right. Go have a good meal and have some fun." She gave him a pat and watched him lope down the path toward the unsuspecting couple who were no longer her friends. Julie turned and continued her trek towards the house, wondering which one of them was going to be killed outright and which one was going to be eaten alive.

Julie didn't have to wait long before the answer came to her on the wind. Miss "I never scream at anything" Kirsti was screaming to put Jamie Lee Curtis to shame. "And that's how the monster really works." Julie grinned, listening to the screams of her former best friend.

The VIP Treatment

RAYMOND AND KIM walked through the Vegas airport. Despite traveling first class and having a decent flight, they were both tired and cranky at the crush of humanity around them invading their personal space. This was their first vacation to Las Vegas and even though all of the slot machines and TV screens screamed for their attention—or perhaps because of it—all they wanted to do was get their bags, get to their hotel, and have a little bit of quiet privacy.

Kim nudged Raymond as they searched for the carousel that would deliver their bags to them. "Look. Do you think they mean us?"

Raymond looked up and saw a pair of young men dressed in black suits; one blond, one brunette. The brunette was holding a sign that said, 'FIRST CLASS - V.I.P. - LUXOR' on it. He shrugged, "Can't hurt to ask." He walked over to the pair with his wife in tow and said, "Hi. I believe you are looking for us?"

The blond man smiled respectfully, "Did you fly first class and do you have a VIP package at the Luxor hotel?"

Kim and Raymond nodded.

"Wonderful. My name is Patrick and this is my trainee, Michael, as we go along, I'll be explaining what I am doing to him. I hope you don't mind?" Patrick glanced at their faces for an answer. After Raymond and Kim nodded their agreement, he continued, "Good. If you don't mind, may I see your plane ticket stubs?" He leaned over to Michael, "You must verify that they are first class ticket holders before you assist them. That is your number one priority."

After confirming the ticket stubs, Patrick nodded. "Welcome to the All-In Limo Company. We're in a partnership with the Luxor Hotel as well as many other hotels on the strip. We pick up the hotel VIPs, gratis, and show them around Las Vegas before dropping them off at the hotel. During the morning, such as it is now, this is to help with the check-in times and allow the hotel to make sure your rooms are ready." While Patrick talked, he and Michael assisted the couple with their bags, making certain that neither Raymond nor Kim needed to lift a finger to retrieve or carry them to the waiting car.

As Patrick escorted Kim into the limo, he said, "Michael is calling ahead to the hotel to let them know you are on your way. They may ask us to delay you briefly. If that is the case, would a quick visit to a scenic view of the Las Vegas Strip suit?"

Raymond nodded. "Yes." He sat back and helped himself to the mini-bar. He could get use to this. Special treatment was the norm for him, but special treatment in unexpected places, such as the Las Vegas airport, was a treat. The All-In Limo Company had something with this current ad campaign. A kind of 'try us before you buy us' deal. He made a mental note to make sure to ask which hotels this company did business with and what their rates were. All in all, it was a clever idea for delaying early travelers while advertising the limo company.

Once they were on their way, Kim leaned forward, "How long have you been working for this company?" Her question was directed at Michael.

Michael paused, looked at Patrick who nodded his assent, and smiled at her. "About a week and a half, ma'am."

"Do you like it?" Kim didn't really care whether or not he did. She was just passing the time.

"I do. It's a little hard to get used to, but the work is easy and the tips are good."

She nodded, thinking if all the passengers were paying was the tip, they had to be pretty good. "Where are we going again?"

"To a small scenic view of the Strip. You'll be able to take pictures of it from there. Pictures that most people don't get a chance to get." Michael glanced back at her a couple of times.

"Will there be a lot of people there?"

Patrick, driving the car, cut in, "No ma'am. It is fairly secluded. A good place to get away from everyone."

"Good. There are too many people around here for my liking." She ended the conversation as she sat back and said no more.

Raymond watched the city and the sky roll by; his mind was miles away on the latest business merger. When they stopped, he looked around. It didn't seem very scenic to him and he hoped to hell these glorified taxi drivers weren't expecting he and his wife to hike up to some ridge for a photo neither of them really wanted to take. "Are we here?"

"Yes, sir." Michael said. "End of the line."

Patrick turned around in his seat, brought up the .38 revolver and wasted no time bantering before he pulled the trigger twice, putting a shot between each of his passenger's eyes. Both fell back in the limo and didn't move again.

"How many times have I told you, "Don't banter with the marks." Huh? I agreed to mentor you, not to put up with your idea of chit-chat." Patrick looked annoyed. "What, do you think you're clever with your little "end of the line" hint? You weren't. Rich people are stupid. Traveling rich people are stupid and dense. They didn't get it. The only thing they're good for is the capture, the kill, and the loot. Got it?"

Michael lowered his eyes and nodded. "Sorry. Got it." He waited until Patrick got out of the car to silently continue his rehearsed monologue that he didn't dare say aloud towards their dead marks. *"Welcome to Las Vegas, chumps. Welcome to the All-In Limo Company—where you get the VIP treatment before you're all-in with us and every ride is a one-way trip."*

The Harpsichord

MONICA CAUGHT HER breath at the sight of the exquisitely preserved 17th Century Flemish harpsichord. It was a once in a lifetime find for a Collections Manager at a local museum. Usually, this sort of visit involved an old family piano that has been passed as their owners died off one by one and it was now in possession of someone who would just like to "get rid of it." But, as these things go, they had a problem finding someone to take it. Local museums were usually a last resort for Grandma's old piano, Aunt May's salt and pepper shaker collection or, if she was really lucky, Aunt Mabel's complete china set. But this? This was different.

"Beautiful, isn't she?"

At first, Monica thought the old woman was speaking to herself. Then, she realized that Ms. Hettinger was doting on the harpsichord.

"Yes. It's amazing. Are you sure you want to donate this to the museum, Ms. Hettinger?"

"Sigrid, please. Yes. I've no family, no children. I would like my darling to go to a good home. One that I know will take care of it."

"Sigrid." Monica confirmed and looked closer at the well cared for instrument. She was delighted by the small embroidered bench standing before it. The intricate design was so pretty, she almost couldn't believe that people actually sat on the bench to play the harpsichord. "We certainly will. This will be, my goodness, the pinnacle of our musical instrument collection." She reached out and gently touched the wood.

"Would you like to play it?"

"Oh! No. I couldn't." She snatched her hand back like a child caught playing with Mom's special occasion jewelry.

"You could." Sigrid gazed at her with a strange greed. "These old hands don't play so well anymore. I'd love to hear it played again."

"But, I don't know how to play." The idea of playing an instrument from the 1600's both fascinated and repelled her. The last thing Monica wanted to do was break the find of her career. This could be the piece that would get her promoted to a bigger and better museum; one where she didn't have to do everything for herself. She could already see herself in a museum with enough people where she could manage others doing the grunt work while she circulated with the local rich, coaxing bigger and bigger donations out of them.

"I could teach you. Or show you. Just a little tune from my childhood. Please. It would mean so much to me." Sigrid sighed at her wrinkled hands. "I hate getting old. They say youth is wasted on the young and that is so true."

"It happens to the best of us." It was an old story, told by many different people: the regret at the loss of flexibility, memory, and looks. It wasn't a conversation Monica wanted to have—again. "Okay. I would be happy to learn this tune from you if you like." It was the least she could do for the woman who was going to make her career for her. She looked at the embroidered bench. "Is it alright to sit?"

"Yes, yes, dear. It's held me for many years. Just sit and place your hands on the keys."

Monica did, alert for signs or sounds that the little bench might break. She relaxed when it held her with solid ease. "Now what?"

The old woman came up behind Monica and reached around her from behind. "Put your hands here. Splay your fingers. Close your eyes and feel."

Monica did as she was bid and allowed herself to be moved. Sigrid guided Monica's hands then placed her own on top of the younger woman's.

"Now, we play this." She pushed Monica's fingers, which, in turn, pushed the harpsichord keys.

The two women plinked out the tune in an awkward cadence the first time around. Then again and again. The tune came out more smoothly with each iteration. It was a beautiful and simple tune; the kind you find yourself humming without realizing it.

Monica realized that she was playing the tune by herself. Then, she wasn't playing anything at all. Instead, she was standing and didn't know how she had gotten that way. She opened her eyes and everything was different.

She looked at herself playing the harpsichord. Monica stumbled back a couple of steps and watched herself finish the tune, turn around, and open her eyes. "Is everything all right?"

"What? What's happening to me?"

"Why, you're old, Monica. I'm sorry. It happens to the best of us." Her body spoke and moved without her.

Monica looked around and saw Sigrid's visage looking back at her from the mirror. "No! I can't. I'm only thirty."

"Now, you're almost seventy."

"I can't be. This isn't possible." She shook her head, waves of old woman hair haloed out around her face.

"And, yet, it is." There was a cold familiarity to that statement.

"You can't. My life…" Monica felt the sudden numbness in her arm and the pain in her chest. "I'm young."

"No. You're not. Not anymore and it's my life now." Sigrid clapped her hand. "So much to do. Wait for you to die—because you will—call the ambulance about your heart attack, become the grieving friend whom you have left all of this to and then, because

I'm so traumatized at your death, pack up and move on to some place new. So much to do! There's just no rest for the wicked."

Monica slumped to the floor, grasping at her heart, struck as much by the maliciousness in that voice as by the pain in her chest. "You can't! It's my body!"

"I already have and there's nothing you can do to stop me."

The two women locked eyes and Monica knew that the thief of her life was right

.

Red and White and Bad for Your Heart

"**WHAT'S RED AND** bad for your teeth?" Shannon's mischievous grin split her face.

I groaned. "Not this again, please? You know I hate them. We've talked about this before."

She ignored my plea. "A brick to the mouth!"

Shannon was so pleased with herself, I thought I was going to punch her in the face. I didn't say anything. I turned away, annoyed, knowing if I gave her any encouragement, she'd continue with her asinine, punster jokes.

"What's a deer without an 'i'?"

I refused to answer her.

"No ideer!"

I winced then dug into my purse. I pulled out a set of needles I'd prepared for just this eventuality. Each needle was wrapped in red and white thread.

"What's a deer without an 'I' and no legs?"

I blinked and looked up at her. I couldn't figure out where this one was going.

"Still no ideer!"

I rocked back in pain as Shannon crowed with laughter. Part of me had to admit, that one was actually pretty good. "If you keep it up, I'm going to have to do something drastic."

Unperturbed by my threat, she grinned and said, "Knock knock."

I sighed. "Who's there?"

"Ya."

"Ya who?"

"Never mind. I prefer Google."

"That's it. I'm done and so are you." I reached into my purse and pulled out a small doll. It was made from soft fabric and sewed with yellow gold thread.

"Awww. Don't be that way." Shannon tilted her head and batted her eyes.

I ignored her flirting. "What's red and white and bad for your heart?"

She grinned then shrugged. "I don't know."

"A needle wrapped in white thread stained with your blood." I held it up, displaying it, before I stabbed it into the doll where the heart was. Shannon gave a gasp of pain and doubled over as she grabbed her chest. "Especially when plunged into an effigy stuffed with your hair." I stabbed the doll with a second thread wrapped needle.

Shannon collapsed to the floor. "Please…"

I shook my head. "You brought this one on yourself." I raised the third needle high. "Third time's the charm."

She screamed and convulsed as this needle struck home. I held the doll and watched Shannon writhe on the floor. When I decided she'd had enough pain, I pulled each needle out one by one. Shannon lay still, unconscious.

I debated about not calling an ambulance this time, then decided that I couldn't take care of all her animals while the house was in chaos over her death. Even as I dialed 9-1-1, I knew she wouldn't remember this. I also knew the next time I punished her this way, it would be the last. As I'd said before, the third time was the charm, or this case, her death.

Perhaps I should think of another way to keep her from telling me horrible puns and jokes.

Five Minute Stories

Volume Two

Finishing Touches

STEPH STOOD IN Heather's studio. The scent of paint, oil and turpentine permeated the air. In Steph's mind, this was how an artist's studio should look. She liked to visit the studios of the artists she intended to buy from. It told her about the painter and allowed her to buy masterpieces at bargain prices.

She stood in front of a piece of abstract art. It fascinated her. It was black and white marbled with splatters of dark red across it.

"Do you like it?"

Steph smiled at the hint of insecurity in Heather's voice. This would be an easy purchase. Pet the artist's ego enough but not too much. Offer about half of what the painting is really worth, then hesitate and rethink it. She would go for the price. "I do like it. It's... unusual. What's it called?"

"It's the first in a new series. I'm calling it my 'Homicide' series."

"There's more?" Steph glanced over her shoulder at the woman cleaning paintbrushes.

"Two. Both smaller."

"I want to see them. Can you hang them up beside this one?"

"Sure." Heather went into the other room and returned with two smaller paintings. She hung them up next to the larger one, just below eye level.

After staring at the three paintings for a few moments, Steph realized something. "These are a set; a triptych!"

"What do you mean?"

"The red paint splatters. They're in line with each other. You splattered them all at the same time."

Heather grinned. "Not many people would notice that. But they don't have to be sold as a set. Each one stands on its own."

"I know. But, I want the set. I like the idea of a 'Homicide Triptych' on my wall. How much for the three of them?" Heather hesitated and Steph didn't like that. She turned to the artist, her game plan shattered. She wanted these paintings so badly she almost ached for them and she didn't know why. "How much for all of them?"

"I'm sorry, but they aren't ready for sale. I still have work to do on them."

"Work? What work? I like them as is."

Heather shook her head. "They aren't done. I can't sell them until they're done."

Steph turned back to the paintings and stared at them, looking for the flaw that Heather saw. She saw none. Artists were such an annoying lot. Dissatisfied perfectionists when they already had perfection before their eyes. They were perfect to her and she was the buyer. Insecure artists be damned! She crossed her arms. "I'm not leaving without these paintings."

She listened to Heather move about the room and come up behind her. Heather didn't speak. The two of them waited in silence until Steph lost the stand-off. "Well?"

"Well, what?" Heather asked.

"How much do you want for…?" She turnedto face Heather and stopped as she saw Heather with a baseball bat cocked and ready for a swing. "What?" was all she had time to say before Heather did exactly what she looked like she was doing and hit Steph in the face. Blood flew from Steph's broken jaw and crushed nose to splatter on the wall behind her. Wounded noises mewled from what was left of Steph's mouth as she stumbled about and fell against the chair.

"Beautiful." Heather murmured looking from Steph to the paintings on the wall now splattered with Steph's blood. "Just a few more finishing touches..." She shifted Steph into position on the chair before bringing the bat down with her full force, splattering blood everywhere—though, most importantly, on the paintings. "Just a few more touches and they'll finally be ready."

A Grave Mistake

DETECTIVE FULLER STEPPED aside as a young man in his late 20s blindly walked out the door trying hard to look like he wasn't crying. The detective felt sorry for him. The death of a loved one deserved tears—no matter what society taught its men. He turned his attention back to the task at hand and entered the autopsy room of the morgue.

Stepping inside the cold room where the murdered woman's body was discreetly covered to her neck, hiding the gaping wound that displayed an empty chest cavity, he asked, "Was that the husband?"

His partner, Detective Monroe, shook her head. "No. The boyfriend."

He felt his stomach drop. "Shit. That means this isn't our guy."

"No. No. It's the Wife Killer. According to the autopsy, it's the same guy; same M.O. The victim was bound by the wrists, ankles, and waist. Her sternum was cracked open and both her lungs and heart were removed with surgical care."

"But, she wasn't married. That's out of profile for him. Do you think it's a copycat?"

She shook her head. "No. Not a copycat. I think he made a mistake. When it hits the papers, it may become our big break. He killed the wrong woman. The guilt may consume him and bring him in to confess." She turned to the coroner standing with respectful silence for them to be done and gone. "Would you give me her personal things?"

The man turned around, chose a box, and handed it to her. Then, he returned to his post, standing silent vigil over his small and somber domain.

Detective Monroe picked out a simple silver ring with a latex-gloved hand. "She was wearing this."

"I thought you said she wasn't married."

"She's not. But, she'd been returning from a road trip."

"So?"

"When I used to travel, I always wore a ring that looked like an engagement ring or a wedding ring. It was safer that way. It told people that you would be missed if something happened to you. It told them that you were in regular contact with someone and it told them that you were not there to be hit on. It's just something single women often do. Besides, I've noticed that I am treated with more respect when I wear such a ring. That's what she was doing here. Her boyfriend confirmed it."

"Damn. Bad luck for her. If she hadn't been wearing it, he would never have touched her. He preys exclusively on married women."

Detective Monroe dropped the ring back in the box of personal effects and turned. The attentive coroner was there to receive it without prompting.

"Yeah. Bad luck for her. I hope to God its good luck for us."

Detective Fuller nodded. "C'mon. Let's get out of Aaron's hair and let him finish up here. I'm up for coffee and I'm buying."

"Ok." She covered the victim's face and nodded to the coroner. "Thanks."

Aaron, still holding the small box of the victim's things, nodded back to her. He waited until both of the police officers left before moving. Then, he put the box back in its place and stepped up to the body. With trembling hands he lifted the white linen sheet from her face.

"I am so sorry," He whispered to her. "I thought you were mine. I was wrong. I did make a mistake." His tears splashed to her slack and pale gray face. "I don't know what I'm going to do to make it up to you. I'll think of something. I promise."

He bent down to kiss away the tears that now seemed like hers. After a final kiss to her unresponsive lips he straightened up, re-covered her face, and wiped the tears from his own. He had some serious thinking to do tonight. He couldn't make another mistake like that again.

Questions

"**WHAT WOULD YOU** say if I told you I know why you like having these sushi dates with me?"

"I would say I was intrigued." He dipped the last of his tuna roll into the wasabi and soy sauce concoction.

"It's because I ask you questions. Lots of them."

He didn't say anything. He frowned then put the roll into his mouth, savoring the taste.

"I know just how important questions are to you. They're your life."

The tuna roll, half chewed, went down hard. "Why...?"

She raised a hand. "Don't waste your precious food. Let me ask the questions. Why would I say that? Why would questions be your life? How do I know?"

He nodded, tense and uncomfortable at this unexpected turn of conversation.

"You aren't the only supernatural in the room. Hell, we aren't the only supernatural creatures in this restaurant. It took me awhile to understand you chose this place simply because you liked the sushi and not because you were comfortable here on a creature level." She glanced at him, feeding on his fear, surprise, and wonder. "Would you like to know more?"

He nodded again, covering his sudden need to flee in a veneer of nonchalance. He took a large bite of *maguro nigiri* as he sucked her question down. Questions tasted especially good with raw tuna.

"How do I know? I know because I can feel you fill with every question I ask you. It can't be the everyday 'How are you?' variety of questions. Though, I sense those are like licks of icing. Sweet, but not filling. Except, I also know the emotional context of the question gives it weight. Isn't that so?"

"Yes." He admitted. "It's like a spice or a sauce. Sometimes, it's what makes the meal." He sipped his tea, watching her over the rim of the cup.

"More questions. I feel your curiosity. Let me guess. Why am I telling this? What will I get out of it? Am I going to hurt you? What am I? How many more questions can I pack into this conversation?"

He laughed a little, savoring the weight of the food she provided. "Well, yes."

"Shall I answer them?"

"Please. This is a new experience for me."

"I'm telling you this because I enjoy our conversations. I enjoy how you feel and taste. I nibble off bits of emotion here and there. You never notice they're gone. Just as you feed from me with every question. I feed on every feeling my questions and our conversation generates. Will I hurt you? No more than I have in the past three years. Have I hurt you? No. Why would I hurt someone I enjoy being with so much? Our conversations are just between you and me. I hoard them. They're mine. I savor every word and every not-word we share. I don't know what I am except a mostly benign predator. Though, I've met others of my kind who aren't so nice about what they do."

"That's not quite true."

"What isn't?" It was her turn to be surprised.

"Why you're telling me this? Tell me the real reason."

She grinned. "Sharp as ever. You're so controlled. Do you realize how interesting a person's fear tastes if they rarely have it? Ambrosia. Yes. I wanted to taste your fear and surprise. I think... I wanted you to understand about me. Also, I wanted you to walk away from our sushi dinners without feeling so guilty. Last week, it was a bit much. I don't need your guilt. I don't want it. It doesn't taste good. Plus, this revelation will flavor all of our conversations in the future, won't it? I know what you are. You know what I am. You know that there are more like us out there. You're no longer alone. How will our relationship change?"

He nodded. "Thank you for admitting that. For being truthful. I'm curious. About a lot of things."

"I know."

"But, I need time to think about it. This. Us. It's new."

"All right. I'll treat tonight. I'm not done eating. I'll be here next week. Usual time. Will I see you?" She nibbled at his insecurity and fear before it could blossom into something too much for him to handle.

He stood and nodded. "Probably. You've got my attention. My real attention. That doesn't happen often." He bent over and gave her a quick half hug.

"Have a good evening." She watched him walk out of their favorite sushi bar, smiling. This time, it had gone so much better. She had had this conversation with him three times in the last three years. This time was the first time his fear didn't spike into terror and anger. This time, he trusted her enough to listen.

"Will I have to fix him again?" The sushi chef asked as he passed her more *unagi nigiri.*

She shook her head. "No. Leave his memory the way it is. I think he's finally ready to join our world. Besides, he has questions and I know how to answer them while he eats his fill."

The chef nodded. "Good. It's about time." He didn't feel it necessary to tell her that he'd helped the situation along with an attitude adjustment or five. Three years was a long time to coddle someone.

Overheard

"**HAVE YOU NOTICED** all the bear statues all over town?" Sam asked his sister, Tonya.

"Huh? No." She munched on her fries.

"Seriously, there are bear statues everywhere. Bronze ones."

She smiled and gestured to the restaurant. "Well, we are at the Black Bear Diner. Makes sense that they've decorated with bears."

He made an impatient noise. "No. Not just here. I mean all over. At most of the strip malls and all of the parks. I noticed it a few weeks ago. So, I started taking notes. I've found a pattern in them. Sorta. Wanna see?"

"Sure." Hers was the complacent tone of an indulging sibling. "All right." She watched as Sam dug through his backpack and came up with a city map; the kind of map a visitor would find at city hall or a welcome center. He had written things on it.

"Okay. See here? All of these marks are where the bronze statues are. They're different than the advertisement bears like the ones outside the diner. But, you see, there are a lot of bronze statues and a lot of businesses with a bear in their name or in their advertisement. I don't think that's normal. Also, see that everywhere there's a bronze statue, there's a lot more bear motif businesses." He paused, looking at her. "Am I making any sense?"

She put down her soda and stared at the map. "Huh. That's weird. You're right. Plus, you have way too much time on your hands." She laughed.

"Tonya, I'm serious. Look again and look for the real weirdness."

She saw how much this meant to him and sobered. She took the map from him and studied it for real this time. He was right on all accounts. Except for one. "What about this? Based on your research, shouldn't there be a statue there? All I see is small park." She tapped the map with one manicured fingernail.

Sam grinned. "You're right. There are bear businesses all around it. There should be a bear statue there. It's, like, the center of everything. But, I've been by there. It's a park and heavily wooded." He flushed as he paused. "I didn't want to go there alone. If I'm right, it's going to be a special statue. You wanna go with me?"

His question was really a plea and Tonya could rarely deny her brother anything. Besides, now she was curious. "All right. But we have to be home in a couple of hours. We'll go and look for the statue." She signaled for the check and paid for it by credit card. Sam practically vibrated out of the restaurant as they left.

A few moments after the siblings left the diner. The man at the table next to them reached over and picked up the credit card receipt. He studied it for a moment before nodding to himself. He returned the receipt to the table, paid for his own meal in cash, and left. As he did, he pulled out his cell phone.

"Max? Yeah. It's Loren. I think we have a real special one here. Just moved into town, but felt a connection to the bears. He might be the one we're looking for." He paused. "Sam Ashton. He and his sister, Tonya, are headed to Ursa's Park right now. You should go have a look at them. He might be the one." Another pause. "Yeah. No. The girl's nothing special. I don't think. Could be wrong. Might make a good sacrifice, but I'll let you be the judge of that. It's the boy I'm interested in. Him, his map, and what he thinks is going on." Loren nodded to himself, listening to the voice on the other end. "Okay. You do that and keep me up-to-date."

Listen to Me

DAN READ THE note Jim left for him on the kitchen counter and smirked.

Dan,

I left the mushrooms marinating in my secret sauce. Use them for the mushroom puff pastries. There are thirty mushrooms. Six for each pastry. No extras, so don't eat any!

Love,
Jim

Dan balled up the note and tossed it to the trash. "Right." He got to work on making the rest of the puff pastry fixings and shells. The button mushrooms looked good and he kept sneaking peeks at them. With a quick look towards the kitchen door to make sure that Jim wouldn't catch him, he speared a mushroom from the marinade and popped it in his mouth. Damn, it was tasty and no one would know that one of the pastries would be short a mushroom.

A few minutes later, Jim came downstairs, "How's it going?"

"Good. Almost done. All I have to do is stuff the pastry shells now." He placed the pastry fixings into the first pastry shell and topped it with six of the marinated button mushrooms. He started on fixing the second pastry shell.

Jim sat down at the kitchen table. "You didn't eat any of the mushrooms, did you?"

"No." Dan gave Jim a guilty smile, placing six mushrooms on the second pastry.

"Did you? You shouldn't have done that. How many did you eat?"

"One." He speared a second mushroom and popped it in his mouth. "I mean, two."

"You're so going to regret not listening to me. You never listen to me and this time, that's it." Jim shook his head in the manner of a sage parent scolding a child.

Dan snorted. "Why? Are they poisoned?"

"Yes."

The short unembellished answer startled Dan. He looked at Jim's face. "No way."

"Yeah way." Jim nodded and smiled.

It made Dan very uncomfortable. "You're kidding. You wouldn't poison me." Dan put the fork down and started towards the sink. He stumbled on the way there and slipped to his knees.

"Sure I would. Hemlock. Diced up in the marinade. Guessing from how you're reacting, you ate the first one ten to fifteen minutes ago." Jim stood and walked around the table to where Dan struggled to stand again. "I wouldn't bother. If you move too much, you'll end up throwing up and that won't help you any. It'll just get you covered in vomit. You're not going to be able to move at all here shortly anyway. Hemlock causes paralysis along with dullness, loss of muscular power, stumbling, falling, nausea, and the dilation of pupils." He sounded like he was reciting a lecture. "And, of course, death. But that won't come for couple of hours."

Dan could feel the strength in his muscles failing. He knew enough chemistry to know that if he did ingest hemlock he was going to die. "Why? Why would you do this to me?"

Jim picked up Dan's unresisting body and moved him to the living room. He propped Dan up on the couch and sat next to him. Jim shrugged. "Because you never listen to me. You don't hear what I have to say. When you do, you don't take it into account. You don't believe me. You don't ever think I mean what I say. I've had it. No more. Now, you'll listen to me and everything I have to say for the rest of your life. I know you'll listen because you don't have any other choice."

Happy

TONY WAS A happy man. He liked it when he was happy and everyone around him was happy. Even his dog, Scooter, seemed to do better when everyone was happy. They walked down the quiet street of Mariposa Avenue and smiled at everyone they saw. Well, Tony smiled and Scooter panted in his jovial manner.

They approached a young woman with cherry red colored hair. It was obviously not a color found in nature, but it looked good against her pale skin. He bet she was a happy person. "Hello!" He called out to her as she put bags in the back of her car. "How are you?"

"Not good." She called back with a smile.

"Not good?" Tony and Scooter paused.

"I'm good. I'm fine." She waved a hand to reassure them.

"Oh, good." They continued on, but Tony paused. He had to be certain. "Are you happy?"

The girl gave him a quizzical look and nodded. "I am."

"Then, I'm happy." Tony smiled and felt free for him and Scooter to continue their searching trek.

A little while later, they passed by an old woman weeding her front flower beds. She was nodding her head to music that had been popular thirty years earlier. Tony didn't have to stop to know that she was happy. In fact, the old woman waved a cheerful trowel at Scooter and him while singing off key to a Partridge Family song as they passed. Of course, Tony had to do a little dance step for her and that made her laugh even more.

It really made his day when he could make a happy person that much happier. It was like having solar panels on the house and giving electricity back to the power company. He found himself humming the song he heard at the old woman's house and tried to remember the words, "I think I love you... So, what am I so afraid of...?" He laughed to himself as he realized that he didn't know any more of the words.

Then, he saw him: the unhappy man. He was obviously unhappy, standing outside his house, looking at it with a clear sign of discontent in the form of a knitted brow and crossed arms.

"Hello," Tony called out. "How are you this fine day?"

"I'm good," The man said without conviction.

"This here is Scooter and I'm Tony." He stopped and offered his hand.

"Elliot." Elliot shook Tony's hand without enthusiasm.

"Is something wrong?" Tony gestured to the house that Elliot was staring at.

"No. Not really. I just have to figure out how to afford to paint this blasted thing. It needs it and my wife wants it painted. Plus, I need to figure out what color."

"A new coat of paint to brighten any day."

"And to give me both a headache and a wallet ache."

Tony frowned and was unhappy at feeling the frown on his own face. "But, won't a new coat of paint do much to brighten things up?" Tony really wanted Elliot to be happy so he could be happy again.

Elliot shrugged. "Maybe."

After a moment's consideration, Tony decided that Elliot was indeed the person that he and Scooter had been sent to find. "You know, I could help you."

"How?" The question was a dull automated response from someone who was not designed to be happy.

"First, let me see how you have your backyard decorated..." He didn't wait for a response and headed around back to the side of the house and opened the gate, stepping inside.

Elliot followed on his heels. "Wait a minute. What are you doing?"

"Trying to help things."

"I'm sorry, but you can't. Why don't you and Scooter go on your way?"

"I'm sorry, but I can't." Tony turned to Elliot, now that they were in the covered security of the backyard, pulled the silenced gun from its custom-made holster, and shot Elliot twice in the chest.

Elliot gasped and fell over, holding his chest where the blood poured out of the bullet holes. He looked up at Tony and Scooter, his mouth opening and closing but saying nothing.

"You're just not a happy person. You bring everyone and everything around you down and I can't have that. I'm here to make things better." Tony watched while Elliot gasped a few more times before exhaling his last. Scooter went over and licked the man's face.

"Not now, Scooter." Tony said with an absent smile and pulled his dog to him as he put the gun away then exited the backyard. "We need to go get the car." He hummed that Partridge Family song and waved to people as he and Scooter headed back the way they had come. People waved back and smiled. Tony reflected on the day. It was certainly a good one. The sun was shining. He and Scooter had fresh meat to last them a couple of weeks and people were happy. That made him very happy.

Not So Crystal Ball

JANET GAZED AT the balls all lined up in a row. She studied them with an intensity that most do when choosing their tool for the evening's activity. It was very important to choose the right one or psychic goop would slime her and leave her feeling like she needed to shower for days on end.

Of course, her eyes were drawn to the shiniest of the balls. Its color didn't matter. What mattered is what one felt when they touched it and looked into its surface and beyond. Unable to stop herself, she picked up the crystal pink ball that practically glowed with a pearlescent sheen and regretted it immediately.

The image exploded in her head. It was of a very tall, burly man with a goatee. He was sitting in front of a surprisingly delicate looking vanity area in pinks and whites. He was dressed in a pretty white negligee and was very carefully putting lipstick on in the mirror. She could see tufts of wiry hair poking through the thin silk.

Janet put the ball back in a hurry. Not that there was anything wrong with cross dressing, but it was too intimate a thing—especially when the man had no hope of catching her.

Her eyes roamed the balls on the shelf and she reached for the shiny black ball, hoping that it would have a much different feel. It did, but not a better one she realized as her inborn talent took her to another place. This time, she was in a bathroom stall. Janet saw a girl in a skirt and a long sleeved shirt. The girl had a foot up on the toilet and held a blood stained straight edge razor. Blood dripped down her thigh. There was pain, but a sense of relief, too. "No." Janet shook her head and put the ball back.

She sighed and saw her companion had already chosen her ball for the evening's event. Blindly, Janet reached out and touched a beautiful tiger's eye ball. She yanked her hand away when she got the impression of two people having sex. She didn't want to know anymore.

"C'mon," Elli said with restrained impatience, "Just choose one. It's not rocket science. We're gonna miss everything."

"I'm trying. You know this isn't easy for me."

"I know, but they all can't be bad."

"I know. I know." Janet looked over the rack of balls again and one caught her eye this time that had not caught it before. It was a pretty malachite ball. Tentatively, she put her hand on it. There was a sleepy, happy feeling associated with it. Emboldened, Janet picked it up. No real images popped into her head. This particular ball had not been used in a while. She smiled. "I've got one."

"Good. Can we play now?"

"Sure." Janet walked over to Elli and set her things down on the table. As she did, she accidentally brushed Elli's shoulder with her hand. The image of Elli dancing around and crowing in delight came to mind. "Well, shit."

"What?" Elli looked at her with bright eyes.

"Nothing."

"C'mon. You can tell me."

"Nothing!"

"Do I win?"

Janet sighed and nodded.

Elli threw a fist in the air. "Woot!"

Janet sat down on the barely comfortable plastic seat, holding her pleasantly sleepy ball in her lap, muttering to herself, "And people wonder why psychics don't go bowling."

Train to Topeka

"**Here we go,** Mrs. Montgomery. This car should be fine for you." The train conductor carefully steered the little old lady through the car door.

Mrs. Montgomery, a week shy of her 102nd birthday, paused and looked at the one person already in the train car. She was an interesting looking girl who favored black clothing, pale make-up, and silver jewelry. "Are you sure? I don't want to be a bother…"

Juliet looked up from her book at the two of them and smiled. "It's fine. I don't mind."

"It's fine," the conductor echoed, helped Mrs. Montgomery in, and settled her oxygen tank next to the nice old lady as she got herself comfortable. He stood up, straightened his uniform, and smiled a professional smile at her. "I'll come see you at every stop, just to check on you. I'll make sure you don't miss your station in Topeka."

"All right, young man. Thank you." Mrs. Montgomery readjusted her breathing mask. She watched the conductor leave, wondering what he really thought of her as he left. The old lady contemplated the train car and her companion for several long moments as the train shifted into gear before she said, "I hope this breathing thing doesn't bother you, dear. It can be loud."

Juliet shook her head. "It doesn't."

"I'm Victoria Montgomery; Victoria or Vicki to my friends. I would be pleased to have you call me that."

"Hello Vicki. Nice to meet you." She closed her book. "You can call me Juliet, if you like."

"I would." An impish smile peeked out through the wrinkles in her face. "I'm going to visit my granddaughter and her family. They would have kittens if they saw me right now."

"Oh? Why?"

"Why, you, my dear." The impish smile became a grin. "My granddaughter would've taken one look at you and demanded another car for me because, obviously, you are a hooligan." She fluttered her hand at Juliet's gothic clothing.

Juliet returned the grin. "Obviously."

"But, I don't think so." Victoria held her head up high with pride. "I used to be quite the daredevil in my day. I was one of the first female archeologists and the first woman in my family to have a job that wasn't being someone's Girl Friday. For example, that ankh you're wearing, it's an Egyptian symbol for life. I found one myself in 1923 on a dig in Cairo when I was just 18." She dug inside her sweater and brought out the pendant. It was small, gold, and ornate.

Juliet moved across the way to sit next to Victoria. "That's lovely," she said as she looked at it.

"Thank you. I have always worn it to remind myself to live and to enjoy life no matter what comes." She tapped her breathing mask. "I don't always need this." She paused. "I don't think I need it now."

"Would you like some help taking it off?"

"Yes. Thank you, dear."

Juliet carefully took the oxygen mask off of Victoria's face and watched as the smile returned through the wrinkles. "Better?"

"Much better. If I were your age, I would definitely dress more like you than my granddaughter. Your look is far more interesting." She reached out and touched Juliet's black hair. "I would live like you do, without a care for opinion."

"Isn't that the way you've always lived, Victoria?"

"Yes. I've always been a bit of a maverick. I've missed my adventures lately."

The sound of the train whistle interrupted their conversation. Juliet looked up and around "I think this is our stop."

Victoria blinked at her. "Is it? You're going where I am?"

The raven haired girl nodded. "I'm going to be with you all the way. Let me help you up." She stood and offered her hand.

Victoria paused for a moment, then nodded. "Yes, thank you." She stood on unsteady legs and waited until she had her balance. "Should I bring that?" She gestured at the oxygen tank and the mask.

"You won't need that anymore."

"No?"

"No." Juliet held her hand as they walked through the train.

A smile of sudden joyful understanding lit up Victoria's face. "Oh, good. It's a new adventure, isn't it?"

"Yes. For you, it is." They stepped off the train into an unfamiliar landscape.

"I don't think we're in Kansas anymore." She glanced back at the train. "What will they tell my family?"

"That you passed away peacefully in your sleep."

"Is that what happened?"

"It is."

"I can't wait to see what comes next."

Juliet squeezed Victoria's hand. "Neither can I."

The Last Present

LYNN FINALLY ARRIVED home after far too many hours of holiday travel. She usually put her patience on high when it came to returning home from any trip, but after the fourth person physically knocked her aside at the airport, her patience had run out. She left her bags in the hallway and collapsed on the couch, closing her eyes. At this point, she didn't care if she fell asleep there or not.

A loud pounding on her front door startled her back into the world of bright light and hard reality. The pounding came again as she pulled herself to her feet and headed for the door. "I'm coming. I'm coming already." She opened the door and found one of her neighbors on the step with a brightly wrapped package in hand. "Oh, hello."

"Merry Christmas!" Rick said with enthusiasm.

"Merry Christmas to you, too, but it's a couple days past now."

"I know, but you weren't home for me to give this to you."

After a moment's hesitation, she invited him in. "I'm sorry. I didn't get you anything."

"That's okay," he said, still smiling. "Your gift to me is being a part of my humble writers' group. We all really appreciate having a pro in our midst."

She nodded. "I enjoy it."

He handed her the gift box and watched her with an expectant air. Understanding that she would not get any rest until Rick left and that he would not leave until she opened the gift and cooed over it, Lynn tore the paper from the small box and opened it. Inside was a small pendant on a leather cord. "This is pretty."

"It's the rune for creativity in the Norse mythology, not that I think you need it." He paused. "Try it on." He held out his hands for the box.

She looked at the rune. It looked a "less than" sign from math. *2 is less than 8*, she thought, as the amount of hours she'd slept recently and the amount of hours she needed to be on her game ran through her mind. She slipped the necklace over her head and looked at herself in the mirror.

"The cord is designed to tighten to any length. Let me show you." He stepped forward and helped her adjust the rune necklace until it tightened about her neck like a choker. Then, he stopped back and looked at their reflection in the mirror.

"Thank you, Rick. I really like it."

"May this creativity rune serve me well in my future writing endeavors." Rick's reflection intoned the words to Lynn's reflection.

She turned to him. "Is that something I'm supposed to say...?" She put her hand out to steady herself as a wave of dizziness wash over her.

"No. That was a verbal component of the spell." Rick was no longer smiling. His look was a cross between fear and hunger.

Lynn stepped back and stumbled to one knee. "Something's wrong. Can't breathe."

"No. Everything's going right. Exactly like the book said it would." Rick stepped forward, watching her with great interest.

"What book?" She looked up as she put a hand to her throat and pulled at the runic pendant.

"Doesn't matter. What matters is that it's all true. Magic is real and what I've always wanted is about to be mine."

Lynn fell to her side gasping in pain as the rune burned hot against her neck. She was too weak to do anything but lie there, looking up at Rick with pleading eyes.

"What have I always wanted? Simple, Lynn. I want what you have. Something I've always wanted. I want your talent. I have all the makings of a great author except raw talent. You have that. I want it. I'm going to have it." He stared down at her. "And, on top of it, now I know magic is real."

She made one last effort to get the necklace off, but her effort was in vain. As she pulled on it, the rune glowed so bright that Rick had to look away. When he looked back, all that was left was the runic pendant necklace on the floor. He picked it up, looked at it, and put it on.

For a moment there was nothing. Then, as light shimmered through his body he gasped. "Is this how you see the world, Lynn? Is this your talent? Oh, it is." He looked around her house at all of her things, suddenly understanding their inspiration. "Merry Christmas to me!"

Phobias

GINA WALKED LILY through the empty house, showing her all of the interesting features of the home—the window seat, the lofted ceilings, the skylights, new carpet and paint. She seemed to really like it. Then, as they walked through the upstairs, Lily began to jerk and turn this way and that.

"Is something wrong?" Gina asked.

"Did you hear that?"

Gina shook her head.

Lily frowned. "I'm certain heard a voice calling out. Are we the only ones here?"

Gina nodded. "You and I were the only people scheduled to view this home today."

Lily jerked again. "What about that? You had to have heard that."

"No. What?" Gina kept her face as smooth and neutral as she could.

"Muffled cries for help. Seriously." Lily looked at Gina's concerned face and flushed. She shook her head. "I should go. I'm not feeling well. I'm sorry. I'll call you."

Gina knew better than to try to stop her client from leaving. It would get ugly if she did. Instead, she walked Lily to the door. "I'll look around the house and see if anyone is playing a malicious prank."

Lily nodded and lied, "Okay. I'll come back tomorrow."

Gina shut and locked the front door. She picked up her large handbag and pulled something from within it before putting it over her shoulder. With angry steps, she stomped over to the window seat and yanked it open. Gary, a rival agent, lay inside, laughing.

"Did she run out screaming?" He chortled. "Did she question her sanity?"

"This isn't funny," Gina hissed at him. "This isn't the first time you've scared off one of my clients from a house they wanted, but it will be the last." She pulled her hand from behind her back and pointed the pistol at him.

Gary stopped laughing and raised his hands. "Whoa. I was just playing. It's all in good fun and competition. I have a client who wants this place and I'm just protecting their interests."

"By frightening off my clients and by playing on their fears. I don't know how you find them out, but it's going to stop now."

"It'll stop. I promise. Just put the gun away. Christ, it could go off."

"No." She reached her other hand into her purse and pulled out a small clear box. "I know a bit about phobias. I know all about yours. Someone in your office told me a few months back. I raised these guys myself for just this occasion. I looked for something even more poisonous, but I had to settle for these guys."

Gina shook the small clear box at Gary. He cringed deeper into the window seat away from the box. A wet spot appeared on the front of his slacks. "Meet *Centruroides sculpturatus*, previously known as *Centruroides exilicauda*, and more commonly known as the Arizona bark scorpion. While its sting is very painful, it is usually only lethal to pets and small children, but I happen to know you are allergic to scorpions... as well as terrified of them."

"Please. Please. I won't do it again. I promise. I won't." He clasped his hands together, begging.

"I know you won't." Gina popped open the lid with her thumb and poured the ten small scorpions on top of her rival. She slammed the window seat shut as he screamed and writhed. Sitting, she listened to his cries for help, holding the window seat down as she smiled. She put the box and the gun back into her purse and settled in for a rocky ride. "I'll call the police, let them know there's an intruder here. Later, I'll call Lily back. Tell her that I found the culprit, that she wasn't crazy, but just had better ears than me. Then, I'll sell her the house. Done deal. No more stolen commissions—ever."

What a Real Psychic Would Do

MARK PUT DOWN the newspaper he'd been reading and looked at the caller ID on his cell phone. He didn't recognize the number displayed, but answered the phone anyway. "Hello?"

"Hello Mark. This is Madam Leota. I know you've decided to come see me. I've set you up with an appointment for Monday afternoon."

"What? Who is this? What are you talking about?"

"I'm Madam Leota, psychic at large. I have a shop down on 45th Street. You drive by me every day and you've decided to come see me. Since time is tight, I decided to get a jump on things." She tried hard to keep her voice from sounding as bored as she felt.

He was completely unnerved. "How did you get this number?"

"The same way I know about you, your car, you coming to see me, etcetera. I'm psychic, Mark. Really, honestly, truly psychic. Now, do you want this appointment or should I erase you from my books?"

Something in the way she said that gave him pause. He glanced down at the paper and saw his horoscope. It said *Make plans to travel out of your familiar territory and experience a new culture.* "No. Wait. Don't erase me. But, I can't do Monday. I've got a big..."

"No. Don't worry about that meeting. The project is going to be delayed by three months."

"What? How do you know? I've been working this thing for months now."

"And who is the psychic one on the phone?"

Mark didn't answer the question, assuming it was rhetorical.

"All right." Madam Leota sighed a heavy, bored sigh. "If you really don't want to do Monday afternoon, I can shift you over to Tuesday morning, but I wouldn't wait much longer than that."

"Why not?"

"That information you're going to have to pay for. I am a psychic, but I've never been able to scry the damn lottery numbers. I've got bills to pay just like everyone else."

"Oh."

"Yeah. 'Oh.' So, what will it be? Monday afternoon or Tuesday morning?"

Mark thought about it. "Just a second." He quickly checked his work email and at the top of the list was an email canceling the project meeting he was supposed to have on Monday afternoon. "Well, damn."

"Just got the notification of the meeting cancellation?"

"Yeah. How'd you know?"

"Psychic, not deaf. I could hear you typing in the background. I figured you were checking your email. So, Monday afternoon?"

"Yeah."

"Great. My rates are $80 an hour plus tip and you won't regret it. For this first session, I'd count on about two hours. I'll see you on Monday afternoon, 1pm."

"Wait. What's your address?"

"You don't need that. You drive by my place on the way to work all the time. You know where I am. If you really think you need the address, look me up on the web. See you then."

"Yeah. Okay. Bye." But he was speaking to dead air. Mark sat back and looked at his cell phone. He looked through his incoming call list and pressed the SEND button on the number that just came in.

She answered the phone without greeting. "No, you don't need to bring anything. Yes, I'll take a check from you. I know you're good for it. No, it doesn't involve your son, Maddoc, or your wife, Tina. It involves you and your future." Madam Leota sounded irritated.

"Oh. Um. Okay." All at once, a huge worry he hadn't realized he had lifted. His family was safe.

"You're going to think about calling me over the weekend. Don't. I don't work weekends. I have a life, too."

"All right."

"Satisfied?"

"Yes. For now. I have to be, don't I?"

Her voice softened, "Yes. You'll be fine. There's just some stuff coming up that you'll need to take care of. Now, enjoy the weekend and I'll see you on Monday. Okay?"

"Okay. Sorry to bother you. Bye."

"No worries. Bye."

Shadowplay

"**I'D NEVER BEEN** so scared. The power had gone out and the sun was setting. I was running out of light as I ran through the hallways of this very building." Ron gestured to the green painted walls as he spoke.

"Running from what?" Kathy followed along, not really listening or looking where they were going.

In her mind, it was just another one of Ron's impossible stories. She knew enough to ask the right questions when he paused so he could continue his verbal masturbation. He never really talked to her. It was more like being talked at. It was just as well. She put up with it—and him—because she needed him to help her finish her research paper. Ron was good when it came to research but not much else.

"The darkness."

This answer pulled her attention from her wandering thoughts back to her guide. "What?"

"The darkness. I was running from the darkness. It was coming for me. Chasing me."

It was all she could do not to roll her eyes. "Darkness doesn't chase. It's just the absence of light. It's just shadows."

He held up a finger. "I thought that at first. Until it touched me. Poked me right in the shoulder." He reached out and demonstrated.

She frowned. "Now you're making fun of me. I don't like it."

"I'm not. I know you don't like it when it gets dark. That's why I lit all the lights before we came. The basement is really dark, but that's where the files you need are."

Kathy didn't want to talk about her fear of the dark. She shivered. "Okay. Well, what happened? With the dark... that was chasing you?"

He led her around a corner to a set of stairs. "Well, I was scared. I ran this way. Came here. I knew there was a flashlight down here. I braved the dark and ran. I almost broke my neck coming down these stairs."

They entered into a dusty smelling basement filled with shelves of boxed files. She didn't like the way the light in the overhead lamp flickered nor how dim the light in the room seemed after the bright hallway.

Ron pointed down an aisle of files. "The records you're looking for should be in that row."

Kathy walked halfway down the aisle before stopping, "What happened after you came in here… with the darkness chasing you?"

"I found the flashlight." He held up the one in his hand. "This one. Turned it on and turned it on the darkness, but it wasn't enough. It kept coming." He reached out and flipped the switch to the overhead light.

It was suddenly so black she couldn't see the shelf she had been reaching for. The abrupt darkness yanked an involuntary squeak of fear from her. "Ron, the light! Turn it on!"

"I'm just letting you see what it was like for me."

His voice, mild in that 'we're-just-having-tea' tone, was still across the room. He switched the flashlight on and pointed it at her. It blinded her. She raised a hand to shield her eyes. Through the glare, she could barely make out his form.

"I was terrified. I ran down here and knocked over one of the shelves. I dropped the flashlight and, amazingly enough, caught it. I got my back to the wall and watched as tendrils of darkness came for me. I closed my eyes, not wanting to see it and said, "Do it quickly." I didn't want to feel the pain if it killing me. Then, I felt something touch my cheek and opened my eyes.

""Tag." It said. Imagine my surprise. "What?" I asked. "Tag. You're it." I asked if it was gonna hurt me. Now, it was surprised. It told me, and I'll never forget it, "We would never hurt you. We were playing. You are of us. You live in darkness. Every shadow is your friend. Every dark room, your haven. We love you." Then, I felt the darkness hug me. "We would do anything for you," It said. And I believed them."

Kathy licked her lips, "So, the darkness is a good thing?" The glare of the flashlight was making her see things. She swore that tentacles of something were writhing around Ron's shadowed form.

"For my friends, yes. For everyone else, who's to say?" He laughed an abrupt laugh, "Oh, right. I am."

There was something in his tone that made her skin crawl. "I'm your friend, Ron. Right?"

"No. I don't think you are, Kathy. I don't think you've ever been my friend. You only talk to me when you need something. Then, you ignore me. I wanted you to be a real friend. Someone I could really talk with and count on, but you've never seen it. If you have, you've never acknowledged it."

"Ron, please. Please turn on the overhead light."

"Okay. But, I don't think you're gonna like it."

The room was lit again, bright in contrast to the darkness. For a moment she was relieved. He had just been scaring her. Then, she saw what was behind him and screamed. She continued to scream until the darkness flowing around Ron overwhelmed her, swallowing her and her voice, whole.

Ron turned off the lights again, listening to the sounds of Kathy's struggle and pain. He heard the darkness say, *"This is fun. Will we play again?"*

He nodded. "Soon. I have plenty of people for you to play with; people who have never been a real friend to me. Soon, they'll all come to play in the darkness."

Room Service

JOLENE LOOKED UP at the knock and the woman's voice calling, "Room service." She opened the door and let the woman in. The uniformed concierge woman was gray under her reddish-brown skin. She trembled as she stood there. On the tray she held was a box about nine inches square. "Your spider, Miss."

"Thank you…" She looked at the woman's nametag. "Pria. Put it on the bed." Jolene waited until the woman stepped away. "Let me see if this is what I asked for. Just a moment." She opened the white box and smiled at the tarantula inside. Next to her, Pria looked everywhere but in the box. "This is it. Thank you."

"You're welcome. If you need anything else, please call. The Continental is full service hotel." The words were spoken by rote. Pria let herself out of the hotel room without waiting for a tip.

An hour later, Jolene smiled a wicked smile as the man knocked and called, "Room service." This time, when she opened the door, a handsome man held a tray with a red candle on it. His nametag declared him to be Emmet. She liked the way his dark eyes looked about the room then narrowed in on the ritual circle.

"Emmet, I need you to take this candle and put it in the center of the circle. And, if you wouldn't mind, remove your shirt first."

His smile was slow and speculative. "It's like that, is it?"

"It's like that."

"The Continental is a full service hotel." Emmet did as he was told. After he placed the candle in the waiting holder, he turned and gave her a seductive look. "What do you need now, Miss?"

"Hold your arms out. Let me see you."

He did as he was told, even spinning slowly in place. "Do I please you?"

"You do." Jolene pointed at him and he froze in place. "I offer this man to you as your sacrifice."

The candle behind Emmet flared as it lit itself. The flame grew tall and wide until it enveloped the hotel worker in a single bright flash of light. His scream interrupted, Emmet disappeared with the light. Jolene stretched her arms out, mimicking Emmet's pose. She felt the power move from the circle, through her, and into the building itself. Sated, the building pulsed with life.

"Well done," she murmured. Without looking back, Jolene left the penthouse suite, took the elevator to the ground floor, strode through the lobby, and slipped in through an unmarked door. No one stopped her. Down the hallway, she knocked on the Manager's door before she entered.

An old black man in a crisp suit stood. "Miss Jolene. I didn't know you were in town." He offered her his hand.

"Liar." She squeezed his hand once then sat across from him. "Good to see you, Dan."

The two of them sat in silence. Dan smiled and shook his head. "All right. Yes, I knew you were in town. What may I do for you?"

"I'm pleased to tell you that the Continental is set for another... session. Well done." Jolene enjoyed the look of surprise on his face.

Dan recovered. "Thank you. I didn't realize such would be needed so soon."

She shrugged. "I don't make the schedule. You'll want to remove Emmet from your rolls. Where *did* you find such a lascivious man? Also, give Pria a little something extra for her part in this. She really was afraid of the spider. Margaret and Trevor were adequate—neither detrimental nor exceptional. They get to keep their jobs."

The old man nodded and scrawled a couple of quick notes on a notepad. "Anything else?"

"Yes. Have the penthouse cleaned. I'll be staying for another couple of weeks." Jolene stood, her eyes sparkling. "No rest for the wicked."

Dan stood and opened the door for her. "Yes, Miss Jolene. The Continental is a full service hotel. Anything you want, any time you want it." He walked out of the back hallway and into the lobby with her. "Will you be having dinner with us?"

"I think so. I need to make a call."

"Good. I'll have your table set for you." He left her in the lobby and walked with a purpose towards the Continental's five star restaurant as he pulled his phone from his pocket.

Jolene watched him go. The Continental's Manager was a good one. She pondered what it would take to make him a permanent addition to the hotel itself.

That was a thought for another day. The man was still young. Not even sixty, yet, and in no danger of poor health. Not while he was a member of the staff. The required sacrifice made certain that the Continental was a full service hotel for everyone... including the staff.

Five Minute Stories

Volume Three

Bedside Manner

NICOLE WAS ALWAYS careful to consider those in her care as she doled out their medicine. She kept in mind their dispositions, whether they were agitated, overly tired, angry, or more rare, calm and happy. She considered their overall health and weight as well. Sedatives could be tricky business; especially the ones she used. Not enough and her patients would be lethargic but active—a danger to themselves and others. Too much and they wouldn't be roused when they needed to be.

For example, the woman in 1A was very slender and calm—one dose for her. No more. But, the man in 2A was a different story. He had been scowling and grouchy since she laid eyes on him this morning. He was big man and demanding, promising to be very difficult with her and her colleagues if she didn't get his dose just right. She considered his weight and disposition then upped his dosage one more level to ensure that he calmed down and remained calm for the majority of her shift.

She delivered the medicine to all of her charges, just ten in all this morning, with a smile and a kind word. Then, she went back to her other duties, occasionally checking on her people to make sure all was well and there were no unexpected side effects. After about twenty minutes, Dana came up to visit her. "My God, it's a zoo today."

"Not everywhere." Nicole smiled.

Dana looked out at those in Nicole's care. "I don't know how you do it. I really don't. I thought that guy in 2A was going to be hell all day, demanding this and that, and being all handsy. He patted me on the fanny as I walked by earlier, too.

But, look at him now; all snuggled down and comfy. What's your secret?"

Nicole shrugged. "I think it's my bedside manner. I do my best to serve each and everyone individually, talk with them, sooth them."

"You're amazing. You have the patience of a saint."

"Thank you. I suppose it's because I was a nurse in another life. I had to deal with people who were scared and those who were in pain all the time. I got good at it, soothing all of their hurts and fears as best I could. This job isn't much different. Really, it isn't. People are scared or impatient or worried or hurting. I just do what I can to make it better for them and everyone around them."

Dana started to respond, but the sudden insistent chime of a call button distracted both women. "Ah, well. Back into the trenches."

"Good luck."

"Yeah. Thanks."

Nicole watched Dana walk by her peaceful, sleeping wards in First Class and make her way into the hell known as Coach. Never again did she have to work that part of the plane. Not since she got her promotion and received nothing but good comments from her people. There hadn't been single complaint since she moved to First Class. Every one of her colleagues was amazed at her success in that section of the plane notoriously filled with difficult, demanding people. They wanted to know her secret, but she would never give it up. She could never be certain they would understand or be able to take appropriate care of their charges in the same way she did. It was her duty—one she took very seriously.

Happy Anniversary

"**I'VE LIVED HERE** for three years now. Today is my "Welcome Home" anniversary." Gina gestured to her home with a smile.

"It's nice." Craig said. "I like the skylights."

"Me, too. It was one of the selling points of the place."

"How on earth did you get it so cheap?" They walked through the spacious fourteen hundred square foot condo from the living area, past the stairs that led up to the master suite, to the back two bedrooms.

"Made a deal with the devil, of course."

"Sold your soul to become landed gentry, eh?"

She ignored the question. "I can't show you this room because it belongs to my roommate and I respect his privacy." She opened the other bedroom door and stepped inside. Craig followed her. "This is the Kitten Room."

He looked around at the shelves of books, the couch, TV, and video games. "Why is it called that? It looks more like a second living room."

"I know. It was just the room I fostered kittens in. When my roommate moved in, I had to shift my library and he brought the rest of this stuff. We were going to call it the Playroom, but the Kitten Room stuck. Especially since I still foster kittens." She watched him walk across the room to look at her books and knew it was time. With soft steps, she walked out of the bedroom and closed the door.

It was the door shutting that got his attention. She knew it when she heard him come to the door and rattle the doorknob. "Gina? Gina? The door won't open."

She leaned against the door without fear of it opening, even though it opened inward. "I know. It won't open again until my home is done with you." She paused to see if he had more to say. He didn't. Not yet. He would, though. His kind always did. "Also, to answer your previous question, no, I didn't sell my soul for my home. I sold yours. Well, not yours personally. Just one soul a year on the anniversary of moving in. Living in a place as nice as this demands a yearly blood sacrifice. That's you this year."

"This isn't funny, Gina. Open the door."

She could tell that he didn't believe her. Not yet. He would. "No. I couldn't even if I wanted to and I don't want to. I don't like you. You spend most of your time whining and bitching about other people. Never taking responsibility for yourself or your actions. Now, you won't have to. Not anymore."

She walked away from the back bedroom, down the hall until she was in the living room again. Smiling up at the skylights, she said, "Happy Anniversary. May we have many more." That was the cue for whatever it was the house did to her sacrifices to happen.

"Open this damn door! I'm warning you!"

She heard him pound on the door and struggle with the doorknob. She wondered once more about the entity with whom she had struck the bargain. It started with the handyman who had tried to rob her. He had tied her up and blindfolded her before he had gone to the back room to start his theft there. The door had closed on its own and there had been a question in her mind from something she somehow knew was part of her home, *"Mine?"*

She had agreed, furious at the robbery and violation of her safe haven. Then, the screaming started. Just as it was now. She could hear Craig's struggle with whatever it was and whatever it was doing to him. She never saw it. She didn't want to. She just knew that tomorrow morning, when she opened the back bedroom door, the room would be as neat as a pin and her home would be sated for another year. It had worked out for the best for both of them for the last three years.

It took about five minutes of screams, struggles, and something that sounded very much like ripping, tearing, and chewing before everything went silent. All she had left to do was drive to some place with people that knew Craig and those people would magically see him there off and on for the next day before he disappeared for good—just one more statistic in the form of a missing person's report.

Tonight she would come home, light a candle, and have a bottle of her favorite wine in celebration. It was how she always celebrated her "Welcome Home" anniversary.

In the back of her mind, she was already figuring out who would be next.

Good-Bye

FROM: 4258913435
    Darkness darkness is spreading darkness

FROM: 5107724297
    The darkness isnt so bad.

FROM: 4258913435
    Who dis?

FROM: 5107724297
    No one special.

FROM: 4258913435
    This use 2 b my homeboys number. But he died last year. Sorry 2 bother u.

FROM: 5107724297
    Its ok. U ok?

FROM: 4258913435
    No. Miss him. Never got 2 say bye 2 him

FROM: 5107724297
    Harsh. Sure he knows.

FROM: 4258913435
    Dont like it here no more. This life sux.

FROM: 5107724297
    Life isnt so bad.

FROM: 4258913435
    It sux. Want 2 die.

FROM: 5107724297
    No! U cant say that!

FROM: 4258913435
    Y not?

FROM: 5107724297
    Life is better than the darkness Jason.

FROM: 4258913435
    !! Who is this?

FROM: 5107724297
    I miss u 2 Jas but not ready 2 see u again yet.

FROM: 4258913435
    Dan? Dat you man?

FROM: 5107724297
    U got 2live. I <3 u Jas. Knuckles bro. gtg now.

FROM: 4258913435
    Dan that u?

FROM: 4258913435
    Dan?

FROM: 4258913435
    Dan?

FROM: 4258913435
    Love u Dan. Bye.

FROM: 5107724297
    Goodbye.

Nightmare Revelation

JENNIFER WALKED THROUGH the house with her sword at her side and her shotgun holstered. The toys hadn't begun to attack her. Yet. They would. Of course they would. They did every night. It would begin as soon as she opened her niece's bedroom door.

She pushed the door open slowly and looked inside. Nothing stirred. Then, the toys began to move. Small movements. Mostly just looking at her.

There was a bright light in the center of the room and that was different. It hovered there, shivering. Jennifer slowly walked towards the light. When she got near enough to it, it shifted and engulfed her.

There was nothing but a babble of voices and a light so bright it blinded her. "I can't understand you. There's too many of you. Slow down. Please, are you going to tell me how to defeat the evil here? Are you trying to help me?"

There was a sense of effort. Through the babble of voices, individual ones could be heard. "Get out. Get out! You don't belong here. Go away from here. Go away."

"I can't. I have to protect Amanda. I have to protect her from the toys."

The voices got louder, shouting for her to leave. The light pulsed with an angry white malevolence. Jennifer stumbled backward. There was a crunching sound under her foot. It was a tube of lipstick. Confusing, but only for a moment. Now that she was out of the light and voices, she could see that the toys had surrounded her and were ready to attack.

She was ready for them as well. She'd learned to come to this home armed. The sword was out of its sheath and in her hands before she knew it. It came down again and again on the attacking toys. But, instead of becoming dismembered agents of evil, the maimed and destroyed toys became other things—broken bottles of lotion, shampoo, and soap.

Jennifer backed out of the room and fled. The toys had started some new evil. They hid themselves and possessed other things. This was worse than before. She had to find Amanda and protect her. Had to get her to the safe room where she could protect them both from the demonic toys. She ran through the house, shouting her niece's name. "Amanda! Amanda! Where are you?"

She burst through the door of her sister's master bedroom and found Amanda cowering behind the bed in there. "Oh, thank God. Come on. I have to get you to safety. I have to get you away from the toys."

Amanda shrank back from her, shaking her head.

"Amanda, this is no time for games. Come here!"

The sudden movement at the door caused Jennifer to whirl, pulling the shotgun from its shoulder sheath, pointing it at the new threat: A tall, pale man in a duster.

The man raised both hands. "Whoa!"

"Theo! You made it! I thought you weren't gonna come!" Amanda dashed past Jennifer to the man. She flung her arms around him as he hunkered down to hug her.

"Nice to meet you, Theo. But, we don't have time for happy reunions. We've got to get going. You can come with us since Mandy knows you." She holstered her shotgun, but kept the sword in hand and a vigilant lookout for more of the demonic toys.

Amanda and Theo just looked at her. Neither of them made a move.

"Come *on*," Jennifer insisted. "We have to go."

Theo cocked his head and asked, "Is this her?"

Amanda nodded.

"Are you sure?"

"Yes!" Amanda almost burst into tears.

The fear and hatred in her niece's voice startled her. "Mandy? What's wrong?"

Amanda was not looking at her. She gazed at the tall man. "It's her. She's the one who kills my toys every night. She's the one who chases me through the house and then locks me away in the dark. She's the bad person. She's the one!"

Jennifer could only stare, openmouthed. "What on earth?"

"Do you remember what we talked about?" Theo looked at Jennifer with hard black button eyes filled with protective hate.

"Yes." Amanda looked at Jennifer.

"Then do it."

The little blond girl, whom Jennifer had loved since birth, pointed an accusing finger. "I don't want you here anymore. You go away! You don't belong here. Stop hurting my friends!"

"What? Mandy, I'm trying to protect you from the toys. I—" Jennifer's voice trailed off as her sword disappeared from her hand.

"You're the bad person. You're the one killing my friends. You don't belong here. Go away. You're the nightmare and you don't have any power over me. *Go away!*"

The force of the command slammed into Jennifer and punched her through the wall of the bedroom. It hit her so hard that she jerked awake three thousand miles away in her own bed.

Confused and disoriented, it took her a few moments before she realized where she was and what had just happened. She remembered the dream; the nightmare. She remembered the fear and hate in her niece's voice and she wondered if she had been her niece's nightmare for the past couple of months. That was how long she had suffered with nightmares.

Jennifer curled up on her bed, hugging her pillow. She wanted to know if she had been the real nightmare, but was too afraid to call and find out. If it was true, she hoped to God that Mandy would forgive her someday.

Considered a Success

"**What are you** doing all the way out here?" Jim asked as he stuck his head in the barn door. He peered at the pile of stuff on the table in front of Dan.

"Working." Dan didn't look up as he screwed the panel back on the camera.

"Working on what?"

"It's a surprise."

Jim came closer. "Surprise for who?"

"Nobody." Dan glanced up with a half smirk.

"By 'nobody' you mean 'for you, Jim,' right?" Jim grinned at Dan with a look that Dan knew well.

"You are absolutely right, Jim. When I say 'nobody' I obviously mean you." Dan stepped away from the camera he'd been working on and headed to the other side of the barn to put away his tools.

Jim stepped up to the camera and looked at it. "It's a camera."

"Yes. Yes, it is." Dan glanced over his shoulder.

Jim reach for it, "What were you doing to it? I didn't know you could fix cameras."

"Don't touch it!"

Dan's sharp command stayed Jim's hand inches from the camera he had been about to pick up. "Why? Is it dangerous?"

"Yes, Jim. The camera's dangerous. I don't want you setting it off while I'm working on it." His flat tone was almost the one he used for dry sarcasm as he turned back to the tool board to put away the tools he had been using—wire cutters, wire strippers, needle nose pliers, and a small wrench.

While Dan was still on the other side of the barn, Jim quietly reached out and turned the camera towards Dan, then clicked the button. He knew Dan hated to have his picture taken and it would annoy him. Jim grinned like a mischievous child. Suddenly, the camera started beeping slow regular beeps that got progressively faster.

"What did you do?" Dan turned around, but didn't approach Jim or the beeping camera.

"Nothing." Jim put his hands behind his back. There was a long pause while neither man spoke, but the beeping got louder. Dan sighed and gave him a look. Jim grinned. "And by 'nothing' I mean took your picture, maybe?"

The beeping continued to get faster and louder.

"You know, Jim, today is the day you regret not listening to me." Dan took a couple of steps towards the back door.

"Why? Is it a bomb?"

"Yes." Dan stood in the door way now. "I told you it was dangerous."

"No way... You wouldn't make a bomb."

"Yeah way and you're testing it out for me right now. Just like I knew you would. Thanks." Dan stepped out of the doorway and disappeared from sight.

Jim looked down at the camera, trying to decide if Dan was just messing with him or not. Then, the rapid beeping became a long tone. "Oh, fuck me." Jim turned to run towards the door when the beeping tone cut out. By then, it was much too late for him and everything else on that side of the barn.

Outside, standing behind the tree, Dan considered the test a success.

Artist Interrupted

KIM LOOKED UP at the knock on the door. She frowned. She wasn't expecting company. She glanced from her sculpture towards the hallway that led to the front door and hesitated. Her sculpture was at a crucial stage. The plaster was still wet and malleable. To pause now could ruin it. But, the knock came again. More insistent this time.

"Dammit." She muttered and grabbed a towel to clean her hands as she hurried towards the door. "I'm coming! Hold on."

She opened the door and stared at the man before her. He was a strange sight, carrying a bag of fast food in one hand and a pair of running shoes in the other. Over his shoulder was a gym bag that looked very full and heavy. The look of surprise on his face mirrored the one on her own. "Uh... hello?"

He blinked at her. "Is Barbara home?"

Kim shook her head. "There's no Barbara here. I'm sorry."

"Are you sure? I'm David. I'm looking for my sister. I... um... I was going to surprise her."

She shook her head again. "I'm sorry. There's no Barbara here."

David looked even more confused. "How long have you lived here?"

"Two years." She felt bad for the man, but there was no Barbara living here. "Are you sure you have the right apartment complex?"

"I don't know. I'm going to have to call her or something. I'm sorry to have bothered you." He turned away as he dug into his pocket for his cell phone.

Kim closed the door and shrugged. It had been an odd, but harmless encounter. One to mention to friends later with a smile. After a moment's thought, she locked the door and pushed the deadbolt home. Something about him made her uneasy. She headed back towards her art room where her sculpture waited for her. Just as she reached it, her apartment phone started ringing. With a sigh, she picked it up before it went to voicemail.

"Hello?"

"Hey, Barb?"

"Is this David?"

"Yes! Barb? Are you okay?"

"This isn't Barbara, David. This is the same woman you just interrupted by coming to her front door looking for your sister. Your sister doesn't live here. If she did, it's been years."

"I know this sounds crazy, but I recognized one of the pictures in the living room that I could see from the front door. It was an Alaskan landscape picture. I gave it to her."

Kim frowned and looked around. She walked to the window and wondered if this David guy was stalking her. "It's a common picture, David. I'm sorry. You have the wrong place."

"No. Something's wrong. I know my sister is supposed to be there."

"Look. The first time it was odd and amusing. This second time is creepy and annoying. If you bother me a third time, I'm calling the police. You got it?"

There was a long pause. "Yeah. Sorry."

"Good-bye." Kim hung up the phone and disconnected the whole unit from the wall. She was tired of interruptions. No more doors or phones to answer. Period. She walked to her art room and closed the door. She stared at her sculpture, but something seemed wrong with it. Logically, Kim knew the sculpture was not flawed. It was the fact that this David person had upset her so.

But it was flawed.

Its eyes had opened and it was now looking at her. Her beautiful sculpture's face was marred because of the interruptions. "Now look what he did. He woke you up. How can I have the perfect sculpture mold of a woman in repose if your eyes are open? I swear to God, if he comes back, I'll kill him." Kim prepared an injection of a heavy sedative and was careful to get all of the air out of the needle before she stabbed it into the woman's bruised and bound arm.

"There now. Sleep. Be my woman in repose. I need to fix your face now. I need you sleeping and calm." She patted her sculpture's arm. "Barbara is a pretty name. Maybe I will call my finished piece 'Barbara in Repose.' Do you like that?" Kim considered again. "No. What about "Artist Interrupted?" It would be appropriate now that I've got to fix your face."

Her sculpture's response was to agree by nodding its head forward and closing its eyes once more. Then, Kim picked up a small painter's spatula, filled it with wet plaster once more and got to work fixing the damage that man did by interrupting her. If she saw him again, she really would make sure he never interrupted another artist at work ever again.

The Perfect Match

"**I WAS THINKING** about a bird of prey in flight over my upper back." Scott watched the woman as she thumbed through her portfolio of previously completed tattoo work.

"Uh-huh. An eagle, I'm sure." Tonya turned the book filled with fierce looking birds of prey towards him. "Take a look through that and see if there are any in the style you are looking for."

He flipped through the book of tattoos, looking at the work. Her portfolio was impressive. He snuck glances at her while he turned the pages. She looked bored and unimpressed. He wanted to impress her more than anything else in the world. "You know, these are good. You do great work."

"But?" She lifted her head and her pencil from her sketchpad.

"But, I'm looking for something more original. A one of a kind piece, you might say. Maybe something you've drawn?" He gestured to her sketchpad.

"I don't know. I reserve my art for only the most special of people. The tattoo and the person have to be the perfect match. Also, it's not cheap."

"Money's not an issue. I've been thinking about an upper back tattoo for a long time. I know I want it to be a bird in flight and I don't want it to look like everything else."

Tonya eyed him with more interest. "I see. Does it have to be a bird of prey? I've got some bird drawings already done that would go perfectly with your skin tone." She really looked at him. "Yes, it might do."

He liked the sudden interest in her eyes. She was already beautiful, but that spark of speculation as she actually considered him made his heart pound. "It has to be a bird; a beautiful one, but not necessarily a bird of prey."

"Turn around." She commanded without a thought to him disobeying. Once he complied, she took a measuring tape and measured off how wide and long his upper back was. "It might work."

"What might?"

"The only piece of mine I would be willing to ink you with." She smiled a bright, happy smile. "I just have to see if your back and the image is a compatible size. I'll be right back." She paused. "Don't go anywhere." She disappeared into the back room and up a set of stairs.

"I won't." Scott was elated. Not only would he get a one-of-a-kind tattoo, it looked like he had the sudden interest of the girl. He flipped through her portfolios while she was gone. Her work was impressive. She had a wide range of artistic talent with the tattoo gun—from lifelike people and animals to tribal art to delicate flowers to the much more traditional biker skull, heart and dagger type of tattoo.

She came back in a hurried rush down unseen stairs and appeared with her eyes shining. "It's a match. It's perfect." She held a new sketchpad to her chest like a schoolgirl with schoolbooks.

"That's great! What have you got for me?"

Almost shyly, Tonya handed him the sketchpad.

"Whoa," was all Scott could think of to say when he saw the image of the raven in flight on the pad. It was fully colored and gorgeous.

"Do you like it?"

"I love it! I'd be the only one with this tattoo?"

She nodded. "It would be one of my show pieces. You would be it."

"I'm in! I love it. How much is it? When do we start?" He didn't care how much it cost. He wanted this bird in flight on his back. He wanted Tonya to do the tattooing.

"Since it is just the bird and will be one of my show pieces, it will cost about $800 to $1000. I'll start with the outline then do a series of colorizing sessions. Each appointment will be about $200. No more than five. No less than three. I can fit you in tomorrow."

He pondered this then nodded. Screw work. He was doing this for himself. "I'll be here."

"Good. No alcohol between now and then." She smiled at him, her eyes almost glowing. "It's the perfect tattoo for you."

"I agree." Steve wondered if he should ask her out now or wait until tomorrow. He decided on tomorrow. It wouldn't do to seem too eager. "I'll see you then, Okay?"

"Okay." Tonya watched him walk out the door and down the street to his car. "Perfect." She looked between the sketchpad and the man's back. She was still smiling as she closed the shop and practically skipped up the stairs to her apartment. She went to the back bedroom where her masterwork showpiece hung. It wasn't finished by a long shot, but it was getting close.

"Soon." She stroked the smooth hide of stitched skin. Her fingers danced over the edges of the canvas where the hole in her sky would soon be filled. Five months for the ink work. Another seven to let the ink smooth and blend on living flesh. Then, she would skin him and gently—ever so gently—tan his hide with the bit of her masterpiece inked on it before she added the missing bird to her living mural of flesh. It would be the perfect addition.

Ice Pops

"**Remember, the plants** need to be watered every other day. Especially my rose garden out back. Roses need regular watering." Ruby tried to be firm in her most serious voice.

Melissa nodded. "I promise. You'll come home from Hawaii with the prettiest plants and roses around. I'll take good care of them."

"You have the phone numbers of where I'll be if something does go wrong?"

"Yes. I do. Written down. You gave them to me twice. Everything'll be great." She smiled at the old lady. "Go and have a good time."

"You can have people over. Just a couple and, please, no wild parties. I know how you young people like to break the rules, but please don't."

Melissa listened with a smile plastered on her face, nodding and wishing Ruby would just go away.

"Also, you can have anything in the refrigerator or freezer or pantry except for the ice pops. I make those special for the Boy Scout troop that comes by every summer to clean up the neighborhood. Such nice young men."

"No problem, Ruby. Honest. Everything will be fine."

"Oh, I'm probably bothering you. I'm sorry. I'll go now. You're a capable young woman." Ruby hugged the girl and headed out on her week's vacation to Hawaii.

Melissa waited until Ruby's car was down the road and out of sight before calling up her boyfriend. "Hey babe. She's gone. Yeah. Finally. So, I have this house to myself for a week. Feel like coming over and spending it with me?"

Melissa lounged naked in Ruby's queen-sized bed with Greg. The two kissed and cuddled. "I think it's time for our post-coital ice cream." She murmured to his lips.

"I think it is." He got up and strolled naked through the stranger's home that had been his home away from home for almost a week now. Something about a young man walking naked through an old woman's house made both of them giggle. Thus, at all opportunities, Greg walked around naked. Melissa grinned as he wiggled his butt at her.

He returned, speaking before he entered the room. "We finished the ice cream last night and didn't go for more but look at what I found!" He entered with a flourish of two brightly colored sticks. "Ice Pops! Do you want red or blue?"

She sat up. "No! Shit. We're not supposed to have those. Anything in the house, but the ice pops. Dammit. You're gonna get me in trouble."

He came over and sat on the bed. "I'm sorry, hon. I really am. I didn't know. I can't put them back. I snipped the tops off and everything. I was being nice." He looked at the two ice pops in his hands that had begun to frost over.

"It's okay." She sighed. "I'll just apologize and offer to help her make more. She may not care if it's only two ice pops." She leaned forward and gave him a kiss.

"Forgiven?"

"Yes." She could never stay mad at him for long. "But only if I get the blue one."

"Deal." He handed the blue ice pop over and crawled under the covers with her again.

*

Ruby knew something was wrong as soon as she came home. Melissa was not there to assure her that everything was all right. She looked at her plants and they seemed fine, but their soil was dry. Clearly, the girl hadn't watered her indoor plants today. She would have to check on her roses soon.

Walking through the house, she saw the mess left by Melissa and at least one friend. This was not right at all. Melissa was always so careful to cover her tracks. The garbage and scissors left on the kitchen countertop gave Ruby the clue she needed. She headed towards her bedroom next.

She could smell them before she could see them. The scent of decay wasn't strong yet, but it was also mixed with the older scent of sex. She found them curled up in her bed, the ice pops mostly eaten with their icy remains melted and staining her comforter. She gazed at the dead couple posed in a sweet embrace for a long time before nodding in a satisfied manner. "Well, now I know the poison isn't painful and works quickly. That's good."

Humming to herself, Ruby wondered if she would even have to kill a Boy Scout this year. She had two perfectly viable bodies to fertilize her rose garden. Or, maybe she should make it only one… to chop up and buried the boy, then call the police and report the murder of the girl. No. She wanted both bodies for her roses. Yes, she knew she was being a greedy old woman, but when your plants became your children, you wanted the best for them.

Ruby laid the plans out in her mind. She would clean up the bodies, mulching them for her garden and clean up her house. Then, she would call Melissa's home and leave a message, thanking Melissa for doing such a wonderful job and asking when she'd like to come by to pick up her pay. It might be weeks before anyone noticed the girl gone. She might even have to be the one to call in the missing person's report. Shrugging to herself, Ruby knew it wouldn't matter. Things always had a way of working out for her. More than that, her roses would be extra full and beautiful this year.

Addictions

"**CHRIST! WHAT HAPPENED** here?" Lynn closed the door to Alice's apartment.

Alice was half lying on her computer desk, one hand on her mouse. Her monitor was dark. From the smell of her, the littered soda cans, and the discarded snack wrappers lying around on the computer desk and floor, she had been at her computer for days. At the sound of Lynn's voice, Alice raised her head. "Help... please."

Lynn walked over to Alice, not touching anything. "What are you doing?"

"The game. It won't let me go." She struggled with every thought as she slumped back in her computer chair in an attempt to sit up. Her hand remained on the mouse. "I tried. The more I won, the more I wanted to play."

"Game? What game?"

"The gem game you gave me. But, I started losing... it... when I lose... it eats me."

"Eats you." Lynn frowned. "The game eats you."

Alice nodded, rubbing her cheek against the chair. "When I couldn't win and it wouldn't let go, I managed to unplug the monitor. I can't see the game to play." She looked from Lynn to the dark monitor and back again. "But, it's still on. It won't let me go. You've got to help me."

She nodded. "I see." Lynn crouched down behind the computers and looked at everything. "Okay. I see the monitor cord. Where's the power strip?"

"To the right. Turn it all off." Alice slumped forward and laid her head back down on the desk. However, instead of everything on her computer desk powering down, the monitor clicked to life and the game, a simple, competitive match-three-of-a-kind game, flickered into view. Alice looked at it with exhausted horror. "No. Turn it off. It's killing me. Please, Lynn..."

"There we go," Lynn said with a smile. "I knew something was wrong when you were still alive. You have to finish the game. Or it won't work and it's got to work. I need *you* and *it* to work."

Alice's hand moved on its own, beginning the next game. She didn't answer Lynn except with mouse clicks and pleading flicks of her bloodshot eyes.

"I knew that was the perfect game for you. You're so addicted to video games. I knew it would be easy to get you to play." Lynn went to the couch and sat down. "I have an addiction, too. It's to life and I need a new necklace." She touched her darkened crystal pendant at her breast. "I've lived for a very long time and I intend to continue to do so. But, I need your life force for that. The computer video game has become the perfect collector. When it's finished collecting you, you'll cry a single crystal tear and die. That crystal will keep me alive and young for another twenty years..."

Lynn stopped as she realized that she had lost her audience to the computer screen. She didn't mind. The point of death was always a beautiful sight. It wouldn't be long now.

Undressing & Dressing

ANN SLOWLY BECAME aware of her surroundings. She was standing in a spread-eagle position with each of her limbs caught up in tight leather shackles. She was cold and uncomfortable but not in pain. Not yet. Straightening up, her shoulders twinged from the strain they were under but nothing more. Looking around with dull wits, Ann slowly realized she was nowhere she recognized.

That was when the fear set in.

"What? Hey." She stopped. Her throat was hoarse, dry, and cracking. After a few hard swallows, she tried again. "Hello? What's happening?" She listened.

Silence.

"Hello? Is anybody there?" She struggled against her bonds. They were uncomfortable, tight and unyielding.

That was when the panic set in.

Ann started yanking on the ropes that bound her for all she was worth. She screamed for help and struggled in vain. When she was worn out, sweating and shaking, the lights in the room in front of her came on with a loud crash of brightness and sound. Startled, Ann turned from it with a cry.

Nothing else happened.

Ann looked back towards the room in front of her and saw her older sister, Elli, lying on a metal table. It looked like the kind of table she always imagined in a coroner's lab—large and imposing with a shallow groove to catch the blood as it was drained. This table's drain was simple. It stopped about an inch above a drain hole in the floor. From the look of the brown-red splatters around the drain on the dirty white tile floor, it had been used before.

"You made me lose a bet."

Ann jerked her head around towards the voice. She started to say something but stopped as she got a good look at the person to her left. He... or she... was a little taller than her and was dressed in light blue surgical garb from head to toe. Pants, shirt, backwards overshirt with a front pouch pocket, cap, mask, and gloves. It was his—she'd decided the person was a he—gloves that made her the most afraid. She didn't know why.

"I told my partner." He gestured towards the room with Elli in it. "That you would last at least ten minutes before you screamed. You didn't even last five. How disappointing."

There was another person—another man, Ann thought—in the room with her sister. He was dressed the same way that this man was, only in white instead of blue. He was looking over Elli, checking her pupils and her pulse.

"Now, he gets to do the undressing and I do the dressing. I always prefer the undressing. There is a certain elegance to it. Dressing can be so messy."

She looked back at the blue one, "What are you going to do with me?"

The white one gave a bark of a laugh. "I told you so. Thin skinned and selfish to boot."

"You?" The blue one asked. "Why didn't you ask "What are you going to do with us?" Don't you care about your sister?" He answered his question for her. "Of course you do, but you've always envied her. Wanted to be her. Wanted to know what it was like to wear her clothing." He moved in front of her and leered from behind the mask. "We're going to give you the chance to know."

When he moved away, Ann saw that the white one had taken a scalpel and had run it down the topside of Elli's left arm from the bicep to the top of the hand. Then he had cut around the bicep and started peeling Elli's skin from her body. Ann began to struggle and cry. "What are you doing? What are you doing to her?"

"Why, getting you her skin to wear, of course." The blue one said as they both watched the white one carefully peel down the skin from the muscle in a single glove like piece. "It's not like she can feel this. She'll die. Soon, I think. But she doesn't deserve to feel the pain just because we need to give you a thicker skin to live the rest of your life in."

The white one held up the peeled off arm and hand. The blue one went over, got it and returned. Ann tried to pull away from him but couldn't go anywhere. By this time, her hands and arms were numb.

"See?" He said, showing her Elli's skin. "Undressing. And now, dressing." He reached up and slid the warm wet flesh of Elli's skin over Ann's hand and arm. "Now for the dressing." He repeated. Letting go of the flesh, it stayed on Ann's hand, but fell away from her arm, as he dug into his pocket for surgical thread and needle. "Let's get you all sewn up here."

"Please. Please don't do this. Please. I'll do anything." Ann whimpered.

The blue one sighed a satisfied sigh. "Like music to my ears. Just keep on doing that. That'll be fine." Then he went back to sewing Elli's flesh over Ann's arm. "You know, we weren't sure if your older sister had enough skin to cover you properly. You know, from head to toe." He nodded his head to a far corner behind her. "So, we brought your younger sister, too. Just in case. She's in the other room. We've got to cover you just right. You'll be wearing this skin for the rest of your life after all."

Ann craned her head around to the corner he indicated and saw two shapes there. At first she thought they were mannequins. Then, she saw that they were human-sized people with black thread sewn all over them, up and down their bodies. Finally, she saw that their heads had been completely covered in a sack of skin that had dried to their faces, showing the open-mouthed horror they had gone through.

The two tailors, as they liked to think of themselves, continued to work contentedly while the first girl screamed and the second girl bled.

The Pact

SARAH AND ELIZABETH sat down in the living room with their homemade smoothies, snacks, and primping tools. For Sarah, it was a manicure. For Elizabeth, it was a pedicure. Sarah sucked on the straw, savoring the tartness of the smoothie. She watched as Elizabeth popped a cookie into her mouth. It was going to be a good night.

Elizabeth smiled at her and asked, "Can you believe John's engaged to the psycho no-longer-ex-girlfriend?"

Sarah rolled her eyes before she took a drink. "I believe it. He was a dumb one. But, I guess he's doing well enough?"

Elizabeth shrugged, rubbing a lotion softener on her feet, working it into the skin. "I don't know. We don't see him anymore. If he's not in New Mexico, he's here working. If he's not working, he's there with her. I guess he doesn't care we don't like her now that he decided she's the one for him for sure."

"Not much of a friend." Sarah shaped her fingernails with an emery board.

"No. But he knows we're still pissed about what happened with you."

Sarah paused in her nail filing to look at her. "I'm really glad you're still talking with me. I mean, I wasn't sure you'd want me to visit after..."

"After you dumped my brother, you mean?"

"Yeah. I know you said if I ever hurt him, it would be bad. I'm glad we're still friends."

"What makes you think we are?"

Sarah blinked at Elizabeth's flat response. "What?"

"What makes you think we're still friends?" Elizabeth looked her in the face, her eyes narrowed and expression blank.

"Um... this?" Sarah gestured to them in the living room with all of their girly implements around them. She hoped that this was a really bad joke on Elizabeth's part.

Elizabeth smiled. It was not a pleasant smile. "This? This is just camouflage. I haven't forgiven you for hurting John. Not by a long shot."

"What? He hurt me first. He cheated on me." Sarah struggled to hold back her anger. "He has no right being hurt because I broke up with him." Sarah scowled, not understanding where this was going.

"You're the woman. You should've known better and forgiven him. Men always stray. Besides, we had a pact, you and I."

"A pact?"

"Yes. A pact."

"What pact?"

"The pact where I told you, when you started dating John, that if you hurt him, I would kill you. You agreed to it." She paused. "What? You thought I wouldn't hold up my end of the bargain?"

"You've got to be kidding."

"Nope. You'll be feeling it soon enough."

Sarah didn't know what to say. "You're not joking."

"No." Elizabeth shook her head. "I'm not. You're already dead. You just don't know it yet."

"I don't believe you."

She pointed to Sarah's half drunk smoothie. "*Daphne mezereum*. Also known as *February daphne*. I dumped more than a handful of berries in the mix. I was afraid you'd taste the bitterness, but you like tart things. It worked out."

Sarah gave a juicy burp and felt a burning in her stomach and her throat. "Oh, Christ. You really did. You really poisoned me." She looked around for her purse. She had to get out. She had to get help.

"It's no use. I've hidden your purse, your keys, and your phone. If you're feeling things, it's already too late." Elizabeth bared her teeth briefly. "You should've let John break up with you. You shouldn't have hurt him. He's my baby brother. I have to look out for him."

"Shut up, you crazy bitch." Sarah looked for anything that would help. She took two steps towards the door before she stumbled to her knees. Her vision doubled as the pain in her stomach and throat spread to her mouth and intensified. She tried to get to her feet but she didn't have the strength to do so.

"I know you don't think much of me, but you should know me well enough by now that when I say I'm going to do something, I really do it. I've killed you. You're already dead. When your body catches up, I'm gonna bury you in the desert. You're never going to hurt my brother—or anyone else's brother—ever again."

Rivalry

DARREL AND JENNIFER eyed each other across the kitchen table like a pair of gunslingers on Main Street at high noon. He put sugar in his coffee while she drank hers black.

"You'll never beat me. You may try, but you'll always fail." She glared over the rim of her mug as she sipped, her eyes never leaving his.

Darrel's smile came easy and calm. "You may think so. But, I've got you this time."

"No, you don't."

"Yes, I do."

"No. You don't. I own more of her paintings than you do and always will."

"I know," he conceded. "But, I own the last painting Heather ever created."

Her mug clattered to the table as she put it down. "That shouldn't count. You're the one who killed her."

"Ah. But, it does count. No one knows her death wasn't a suicide. The tragic death of one so young and talented. I can hear the reporters now. "Darrel, as the foremost collector of Heather Drury's work...""

"One of the foremost, you poseur."

He ignored her interruption. "..."how does it feel to know that you bought the last painting she ever created?" I feel so privileged and sad, Marsha. Miss Drury was an inspired artist and a good friend. We'll all feel her loss for a long time to come."

Jennifer have an impatient scoff. "She was going to sell that painting to me."

"I know, darling. Hurts, doesn't it?" Darrel sipped at his coffee.

"I know something that'll hurt you."

"Yes? Then, hurt me, baby." His eyes dared her, calling her bluff.

It wasn't a bluff. "Barb sold me her entire Drury collection this morning."

It was Darrel's turn to slam his coffee mug to the table. "No!"

"Yes!" Jennifer's grin of triumph stabbed him in the heart.

He stood. "That bitch! She promised it to me."

"I know, darling. Hurts, doesn't it?" Jennifer mocked him with his own words and sipped at her coffee. "And that means my collection will not only be larger than yours, it will be worth more. Especially since the painter is now dead and I own more than half of all of the paintings she ever made. There's no way for you to catch up with me. Face it, Darrel; you've always been a step behind."

"You traitorous bitch." He leaned over the table, aching to knock that smug smile of hers into next week.

"Murdering bastard." She bared her teeth in a humorless smile. "But, you do own the very last Drury painting ever made. Be satisfied with it. Enjoy and revel in its status. You don't know how long you'll be able to keep it, do you?"

"You'll get yours, Jennifer. I swear. I'll have those paintings if it kills me. Or you." Darrel turned, strode out of the kitchen, and out of the small apartment. He slammed the front door in a final expression of anger.

"Most likely you first." Jennifer finished off her coffee. She was careful to clean up her mess before she left the kitchen. She let Darrel's cup and spoon remain where they sat on the table—fingerprints and all.

Jennifer walked through the artist's small apartment to the back bedroom. Paints, easels, blank canvas, brushes, and rags were everywhere. There was even some plastic down where it looked like Heather had been about to start another one of her painting binges. Jennifer walked into the back bathroom where Heather's body lay with slit wrists in the tub. She saw that one of Heather's arms hung out of the tub and the blood was beginning to clot on the wrist wound.

"H-help me." Heather's eyes opened and closed as she whispered her plea.

"You're still alive." Jennifer considered the situation. "Clearly, this won't do." She found a box of latex gloves and put a pair on. Then, returned to Heather. Careful not to step in the small pool of blood, Jennifer picked up Heather's unresisting arm, flicked the blood clot off the painter's wrist into the bath water and made sure the blood was flowing once more before putting the almost dead woman's arm back into the tub.

"Please," Heather whispered, too weak to even open her eyes this time.

"I'm sorry, darling." There was real regret in Jennifer's voice. "But, your paintings are worth much more now that you're dead. I have to make sure that Darrel never catches up. It's just one of those things. I don't know if you can understand. But, don't worry; it won't matter for much longer. Just rest now and know that your work will always have a place of honor in my home."

Dust Bunnies

LEWIS GAZED AT the house standing before him and shook his head. As an inspector for the city, he could already tell he was going to have to condemn the thing. Two questions remained: how many things were wrong with it and would the city need to push the owner into knocking it down sooner rather than later.

"You aren't going in there, are you?" a creaky voice from the side asked.

Lewis gave the short, old man a nod. "Have to."

"I wouldn't do that. That house," the man gestured with his whiskered chin, "it eats things."

"Uh-huh. Eats things." Lewis made a checkmark on the left of his sheet. It was his private notation system for the number of people who talked to him and what their disposition was. Left for weird. Right for angry. Top for kind. Bottom for busybodies.

"Yep. Cats, dogs, birds. Nothing goes there now. Not even squirrels. They got wise to what's inside."

"Well, thank you, sir. But I've got a job to do." He didn't dare ask for information. The old coot would give it to him. Probably in long-winded form. It'd taken a couple of friendly conversations to get it through is head that people who talked to inspectors had no one else to talk to. If you gave them an in, they'd never let you go.

The old man shook his head, his opinion clear. Lewis was being foolish. "Good luck, young man. I hope to see you again." He toddled away, still shaking his head.

"Thank you. You have a good day, sir." Lewis put a second checkmark on the left side of his sheet.

That old man deserved it. Muttering to himself, he strode up the cracked sidewalk, stomping on the cracks in deliberate rebellion against the superstition. All the while, he kept a keen eye on his target, examining it for flaws—of which there were many.

The front porch was solid enough, but there were clear cracks in the house's foundation. A quick scrape against the doorjamb revealed dry rot. He used his small pry bar to get the door open. The owner had been warned, through the mail and the multiple notices posted to the door, that the inspection was coming.

Inside was in much better shape than Lewis had expected. Dusty, yes, but neat in the grand scheme of things. He took a deep whiff then sneezed. Dust, yes. Nothing wet. At least, not here in the front room.

As he walked through, the house itself was mostly bare. There was scant furniture. Just one or two pieces in each room. Even the kitchen was clear of food stuffs and debris. With a tilt of his head, Lewis realized that the house had been staged. The furniture had been placed here by a real estate company. He frowned. There was nothing in the paperwork to indicate that the house had been for sale.

It wasn't until Lewis entered the bedroom that he found something out of place. On the floor next to the bed was a woman's handbag. It had fallen over and a couple of things peeked out. He picked it up, gathering the reading glasses, tissues, and lipstick as it he did. All of it was covered in a fine layer of dust.

Looking through the purse, he couldn't find a wallet. He did find a set of keys with a photo keychain of two young children. *She's a mother. They're five or six years old. I think.* Lewis mused on his guess for a moment before putting the purse and his checklist on the only other piece of furniture in the room—a nightstand. He backed up and looked under the bed.

At the edge of his vision, he could see something that looked like the side of a wallet. For a moment, he debated. Did he really want to roll around on the dirty floor to get to it? In the end, there was no choice. He'd wonder about the purse, and the mother of those children, for the rest of his life. If nothing else, he could call the purse's owner and let her know he'd found the purse and where.

With a sigh, he got on his knees and reached under the bed. As he touched the wallet, something wrapped itself around his hand.

With a yelp, Lewis yanked his hand out from under the bed, wallet clenched in a fist. Around his hand was the largest dust bunny he'd ever seen. It was massive with dirty hair wrapped about both the wallet and his hand.

He dropped the wallet and shook his hand free of the dust bunny. Shuddering, he had to laugh at his fear. That laughter stuck in his throat when the dust bunny moved on its own and gave a soft mew. It tightened itself around the wallet. Something that looked sort of like a mouth gnawed on the wallet.

Leather, Lewis thought. *It's eating the leather.*

The dust bunny stopped its gnawing and gave another soft mew. Behind Lewis, something much bigger grunted in reply. Not wanting to, but unable to stop himself, Lewis turned and saw the closet door open. Filling the door opening was a huge dust bunny made of dirt, hair, cobwebs, and stuff he couldn't identify and didn't want to. *It's a parent*, he thought.

The creature launched itself at Lewis with single-minded hunger. It moved so fast Lewis didn't have time to scream. Fortunately for him, he was dead before the dust bunnies started feasting on his flesh.

Five Minute Stories

Volume Four

Diamonds Are Forever

BRIAN PACKAGED THE last of his LifeGem orders with care and sent them on their way. He hoped they would bring solace to those grieving lost loved ones. Then, he closed down the lab for the day. After a light, solitary dinner of Chinese food at his favorite family-owned Chinese place, Brian headed home.

"Hello Cerberus." He greeted his cat with a stroke on the head. "We have a new member of the family." The cat peered at him with intelligent eyes and turned, walking to the basement door. "Eager to meet him, I see. All right. No rest for the wicked."

The basement didn't look like the normal basement of a bachelor—or any normal person for that matter. It was brightly lit with display cases lining the walls, each one filled with thousands of loose gems in many colors. Each display case was labeled with titles such as "Medical," "Financial," "Technical" and "Religious." Others were labeled with words like "Pretty," "Kind," "Hateful" and "Revenge." Looking closer, each loose gem had an identifying card placed in front of it with a name, age, and cause of death. These were for quick reference only. The rest of the information was stored in his extensive files.

Brian sat at his desk, pulled out a file from his filing cabinet, and a small package from his pocket. Cerberus sat on the desk watching. "This is Mr. Marren, my former boss." On a card, he wrote, *Joseph Marren. Age 36. Car Accident.* He rose and placed it in front of an empty spot in his "Revenge" display case. Returning to the desk, he pulled out a small box of ritual implements. Each of which he put on: an ornate necklace, a matching ring and a worn purple sash. "Time for the old boss to meet his new one."

The cat said nothing, but picked up the package, leapt from the desk, and placed it in the middle of the ritual circle on the floor. The cat remained within the circle, watching the specially prepared package. Brian stood outside the lines. He spoke several words of power that few others in the world could understand. The package within the circle burst into flame and a transparent Joseph Marren appeared where the package had been.

"What? Where? Brian? What's going on?"

"Shut up, you useless sack of shit." He savored the moment. "Oh, I have wanted to say that to you for such a long time."

Mr. Marren sputtered in outrage. "Now see here! You cannot speak to me like that."

"Cerberus?"

The cat sprang forward and slashed at the spirit with vicious claws.

Joseph yelped in pain and kicked at the cat. He froze when his foot passed right through the little beast.

"Rule number one: You will call me 'Master.' Rule number two: You will never again interrupt me. Do you understand?"

Joseph nodded slowly, frightened and confused. "Yes."

"Yes what?"

"Yes... Master."

"Good. You're dead. You died in a car accident. Your widow, of course, sent your remains to LifeGem to turn into a synthetic diamond. I took the liberty of making my own gem. You have no idea how much easier it is to keep a spirit around when you have their remains in gem form. No worries of it decaying." Brian enjoyed the look of horror on his former boss's face. "Yes, you're a spirit and now my servant."

"Why?" Joseph looked at his translucent hands and wanted to cry.

"Why not? The technology works perfectly with the Old Ways. It makes things easier. It's the whole reason I became a technician there. It's the reason I put up with you for so long. Where else can a man so easily gather the remains of the dead? A little bit is all I need to work my will."

"You're mad. You can't. I can't be... I died. I should be free. I should go on. Set me free. Please, set me free."

"No. I don't think so. Not until the Second Coming—if it ever comes. I have use of you already. Tell me about your wife. She's very pretty. What's her favorite color? What's her favorite flower?"

"No. I won't."

"Yes, you will. *Now.*"

Compelled by forces beyond his ken, Joseph answered in a flat voice. "Her favorite color is purple. Her favorite flower is the carnation."

Brian nodded. "I think I'll pay her a condolence visit and bring her your other stone. I had it mounted in the bracelet setting she wanted, but didn't think she could afford. Of course, I didn't want to just send it to her in the mail. A personal visit would be so much more appropriate. She probably needs someone to console her in her time of grief. I'll be happy to provide that for her."

Joseph sputtered, "You wouldn't. Not my Elizabeth."

"I would. I will. I'm not a man easily thwarted. Oh, you can come watch me. You can visit your other LifeGem, but you can't interact with anything around it. All you can do is watch. This place," he gestured to the room, "is the only place you can interact with your environment, but only when I call you and send you out on tasks. Be careful, though, Cerberus likes to play with my servants and I let him."

"How can you do this? How can you keep me trapped here?"

Brian walked through the circle and picked up the little purple stone. He placed it carefully within his "Revenge" display case behind the Joseph Marren's sign. "Diamonds aren't the only things that are forever."

Collateral Damage

WENDY RAN THROUGH the empty building as if her life depended on it. The way this game was played, it did. She had the advantage. She knew this building better than her adversary, but it would be foolish to underestimate her new friend. The fifteenth floor, where the goal was, would be the stage for the endgame.

Instead of using the elevator, she used the stairs—after pressing a bunch of buttons as a distraction. She snuck out down the hall, minding her step. In an empty building was under construction, steps echoed and obstacles plotted to reveal her location.

There was no door to the suite that would contain her office and the offices of her co-workers. Just a plastic drape. This was new and even better than she had hoped for. Keeping close to the wall, she snuck around the partitions, the scattered equipment, and the newly dry-walled offices. Every step was an anticipation of being discovered then a brutal fight to the death.

After one last corner, she was in sight of her goal: an envelope on the windowsill with instructions. Quick look left. Quick look right. Nothing. No sound except the perfect movie moment of a breeze rattling draped plastic. No one was in the room. All she had to was get to that envelope...

A shot rang out and Wendy yelped as something hit her from behind, accompanied by a voice saying, "You're dead you know."

Wendy whirled and saw her adversary pointing her hand in the shape of a gun. "Shit. Yeah. Ok. You win. Wait... what the hell was that noise?"

Susan laughed and pointed to the fallen broom. "Just that. I knocked it over to make a sound..."

"... like a gunshot. Fuck. So close."

Susan walked into the room and picked up the envelope. "Now, you'll never know my middle name. Hah!" Stuffing the envelope in her pocket, she looked around the office and at the view. "Wow. This is pretty spectacular. Thanks for showing it to me."

"No problem. I never get to play T.A.G. with anyone. This was a good excuse."

"I had fun. Still, thanks. I know I'm a little weird wanting to see a place before I agree to interview. I just..." Susan saw Wendy looking past her, out the window, towards the convention center rooftop. "What?" She turned around to see what Wendy was seeing.

Wendy stepped to the window. "Those guys. They're fighting. On the rooftop." She squinted, looking at them. "Holy shit!"

"What? What?" Susan craned her head to see as well.

"I think I know one of them."

"You what? No way! Which one?"

Wendy pointed. "The one on the left. He's a friend of a friend from Seattle. I've met him only once, but what an impression. It was like meeting James Bond in the flesh. That's him. That's Ivan. I'm sure it is."

"You're kidding. What's he doing here in Sac?"

"I don't know." Wendy stepped back from the window. "But, I think he just killed that guy."

Wendy didn't have time to register the coughing sound of the silenced small caliber pistol. Two shots to the head and she was dead before she hit the ground.

Susan's happy smile was replaced by a cold expression of annoyance. She checked Wendy for vital signs before checking the window again. Her partner was still there, doing his job.

She waited for his signal then opened a secured line. "Black Leader, this is Red One."

"Go Red One."

"Building secured. Cleanup needed on 15."

"Anything to be concerned about?"

"No Sir. Just collateral damage. One black bag."

"Copy that. Sending the cleanup crew. Radio silence until 1600.

"Copy that. Over and out." Susan clicked off the small radio and looked to the dead girl lying at her feet. "Sorry, Wendy. I know you've always wanted to be a spy. Guess you'll have to be content with being killed by one."

Locks of Love

IT TOOK WHAT seemed like forever for his host to finally go to sleep. He was curled up next to the new lover who was asleep as well. The symbiotic parasite waited a few minutes longer before he lifted several prehensile locks of graying brown hair to look at the new female.

Nothing special, just like the last one. He couldn't understand why his host wasted so much time with these human females. Most of them wanted to change him and made demands. Some wanted him to cut his hair! That just wouldn't do. He wanted his host the way he was. He would have to get rid of her... just like he did the last one.

Had his host been awake, he wouldn't have recognized himself. His hair seemed at least twice as long as it actually was with it fanned out in the air. His host probably would have been horrified to see it... then to watch his own hair slowly descend to wrap itself around the female's neck. He would strangle this one until she woke up gasping for air. She would become afraid and leave.

She...

Suddenly, he was far more alert. There was resistance to the strangling. How could this be? Then, he understood. The human female was a host to one like himself. In that instant, all pretenses were ripped always and the instinct to prove who was stronger dominated. He had the better grip. The other one, a female, now that he was actually paying attention, was longer, thicker, and stronger. Her locks twined about his locks, squeezing, pushing, and pulling, blocking his attempts to strangle her host.

He would lose. He could tell. But he couldn't relent. Not now. Not until it was certain. Once the battle for dominance was begun, there was only one way for it to end: the near death of the host being fought over or the clear victory of the host saved.

Which was exactly what was happening. Her locks, shining red and strong, covered his locks, pushing them back. It was like a silent arm wrestling match with rippling locks of hair instead of the bulk of muscle.

A much smaller lock of her red hair snaked forward and began to wrap itself around his host's neck. At that point, the battle was lost. He went limp; graying brown locks of hair shrinking and lying slack against his host's head and the pillow it rested on.

Slowly, the other one, the beautiful red one, released the vanquished enemy locks one by one, and fanned itself out above the sleeping couple in well earned triumph. It released the lock from about his host's neck last as a reminder that she could have killed his host, and thus, him.

Inch by inch, the warrior queen settled back down; her locks lying against her host's head and shoulders.

It had been such a long time since he had met another of his kind, especially such a magnificent female specimen like this one, that he almost didn't know what to do. He would have to remember the ancient courting rituals. Only they would be worthy of one such as this.

With respect, he lifted a single lock of hair. She was on alert. Two locks coiled up into strike poses. His lock dropped low and slithered from his host's shoulder to her host's shoulder until it was barely touching one of her locks of hair that had not risen up.

With a twitch, his lock was flicked back over onto his host's shoulder, but she didn't strike. It was a promising beginning. He would have to move slow and court her properly. As long as his host and her host slept together, he would have all the time he needed to win her heart.

Interloper

I PUT MY found treasures down on one of the clear spots in the room. The building was silent. Once, I would've said it was an eerie silence. Now, silence was the norm and all sound was suspect. All sound had to be identified for threat rating. Sounds like the quiet footsteps coming down the hallway. I waited and watched the door, ready to respond.

The person paused in the doorway and we surveyed each other. It was my work partner, Rory. I relaxed. "Find anything worth keeping?"

He nodded. "I did. I swept the entire third floor."

"Any trouble?"

He shook his head. "You?"

"I got all of the first floor and part of this floor. I didn't see anyone, but I don't think we're alone."

Rory paused in the motion of unloading his pockets. "Should we move to a more secure spot? This place is an open thoroughfare."

"Nah. Like I said, I didn't actually see anyone. If they're here, they're more scared of us than we are of them. Or, they're a rat." I watched him as he once again started unloading his haul. It was all pretty good stuff: Candy, mostly. All wrapped and untampered with. It was a good complement to my chips and crackers.

"Yeah. Rats aren't afraid of anything." He put his hand to his breast pocket. "You'll never believe this find." He unveiled it with a flourish as he set it on the countertop.

"Holy shit!" I was surprised. "Is that a full sized Snickers bar?"

"Yep."

"I haven't seen one of those in... forever. Where the heck did you find it?"

Rory shrugged. "One of the abandoned conference rooms."

"Sweet." I reached for it, but the room was suddenly flooded with light.

Both Rory and I whirled in surprise and stepped back from our most feared enemy. We stared at her in horror as she stepped into the room and began to speak. I was certain we were dead. A couple of seconds later, I could only wish we were.

"Oh. My. God. Did you see that weather out there? It's so sunny. I can't believe it and I'm stuck here working the weekend." She walked into kitchen without hesitation and continued to speak without taking a breath. "Working on the weekend, too? Sucks doesn't it. But, I've got such a big presentation that's due this next week and I won't be able to get it done and go to both my hair and nail appointments at the same time. So, I'm here now. What were you two doing in here with the lights off?" She looked through the cabinets for a coffee cup and sugar.

Rory and I looked at each other. "Conserving energy," I said.

"Oh. Well, I don't think you have to worry about that on the weekends. It's not like there's too many other people using it. What are you guys working on?"

Rory and I looked at each other again. "The Protégé R-400." Rory said.

"Oh. Engineers." She spoke with a tone of voice reserved for Muffin when he tinkled on the carpet. "I see. Well, I need to get back to work. I have a presentation to give to the Higher Ups." The subtext *'whom you will never meet'* was clearly tacked onto that statement. She got her coffee from the pot on the counter and noticed the pile of scavenged goodies. "Oh, Snickers! I love Snickers."

She took the candy bar along with her coffee and flounced out of the corporate kitchen.

Rory and I stood in silence for a long moment. Finally, I asked, "What the fuck was that?"

"Relentlessly perky." Rory's tone was droll.

"We should hunt her down, kill her, and eat her."

"Yeah, but then I'd get perky stuck in my teeth and I'd be belching marketing strategies for hours. You know how much I hate that."

"Yeah." I sighed.

"She took the Snickers."

"I noticed. Bitch."

"I bought that for you."

I looked at him. "You didn't find it on the third floor?"

"Nah. But it made for a great story, didn't it?"

"Yeah. You did well my apocalyptic minion. You did very well."

He scooped up the rest of the snack food while I got us a couple of sodas. "Back to work?"

I nodded. "Fortified and ready. Back to work. We can play another day."

The EMP Touch

It wasn't every day that one received something from a dead person in the mail. Brad looked at the envelope with some interest and a bit of trepidation. It was from Erin, sent to him on the day she committed suicide. That had been just three days after he walked out on her with her best friend, Diane. He still felt guilty about the incident. Now, he felt even more uncomfortable, knowing that she sent him this envelope on the day she killed herself.

He opened it and glanced inside. There was a coin and a letter. He pulled the paper out, but found that it was blank. He poured the coin out of the envelope into the palm of his hand. Hissed in pain, he dropped both the letter and the coin. As the coin clacked to the ground, he saw that the previously blank sheet now had writing on it.

Brad looked at the palm of his left hand and frowned at the burn mark there. It was in the shape of a coin with a lightning bolt in the center. It hurt. It was at least a second degree burn.

He hunkered down and poked at the coin with a stick. Nothing happened. He held his hand over the coin, feeling for warmth and there was none. Steeling himself for more pain, he poked at the coin with the tip of his finger. Nothing happened. Reassured, he picked it up, a plain silver thing with a lightning bolt on one side, and was relieved that it didn't burn this time. In fact, it was cool to the touch. He wondered how it could have burned him in the first place.

He grabbed the now legible sheet of paper before it could flutter away and headed into the house to read it. The hallway light burst and went out when he flicked it on. His day was going from bad to worse. He walked into the kitchen and started reading.

"Dear Brad,
I thought long and hard on your betrayal and the pain you put me through. I could wax poetic about what an awful person you are to do this to me but, you know me, I am more of a woman of action than words. By now, you have touched the coin and the spell I wrought is complete. When I'm hurt, I don't just get mad, I get even. With this spell, curse to be exact, at the cost of my own life, I have condemned you to live forever. I believe this is a just punishment for you."

He rolled his eyes. This was exactly one of the reasons he ran off with Diane. Erin was always spouting off such insane shit. Who could blame him? He opened the refrigerator and grabbed a soda. While there, he noticed that the interior light wasn't on and he couldn't hear the refrigerator running. Great, more problems. He closed the door, opened the soda, and continued to read.

"I know of your love of high tech toys and I know that you spent hours chatting with Diane on IM and in your game while ignoring me. I decided to take all of that away from you. You know how Midas had the touch that turned everything into gold? Well think of this curse like that, but only with all things electronic and electrical. I have cursed you with the EMP touch. Everything you touch that has electricity in it will be destroyed. In return, all of your aches and ills and injuries will be cured."

Brad looked down at the burn on his palm. It was healed over; a white circle with a white jagged lightning bolt scar. He poked at it and felt no pain. "This can't be happening." He muttered.

"What?" Diane came in from the back room.

"This." He gestured the letter. "It's from Erin. She says that she killed herself to curse me."

"What? You're kidding." She took the letter, scanning it quickly. "Oh, honey, the woman was insane. She killed herself and she wanted you to feel guilty for it. Don't worry about this trash. It was all in her head." She hugged him, kissing him on the cheek.

He held her for a silent moment, hoping she was right. Then, he felt her trembling. Turning, he saw Diane's eyes had rolled back up in her head. She was having some sort of seizure. As soon as he let her go, she collapsed to the ground. He crouched over her, calling her name, trying to revive her. He stopped when he realized that her seizure got worse every time he touched her.

Backing away from her, he fumbled for his cell phone. It sparked and died as soon as he touched it. He ran to the house phone but only heard static.

After throwing the phone across the room, he hurried back to Diane and was relieved to see that she was still breathing, but was still unconscious. He carefully took the letter from her hand, without touching her, and saw that more writing had appeared. He backed away from his girlfriend and read what was there.

"I know you haven't learned the extent of my curse yet, love of mine, but by now, you have learned that my curse of the EMP touch extends to living things. In particular, to humans. I know it takes two to tango and Diane is just as guilty of betraying me as you are. If she is not the first human you touched and she is not suffering from having every electrical impulse in her body going insane, know now that you can never touch her again—or any other living creature for that matter—for the rest of your very

extended life. Not a human. Not an animal. Not even a bug. Each time you do, you will either kill them or cause lasting harm.

Additionally, each time you're hurt, even just the suffering of age, your EMP touch will heal you. It will force you to live for as long as there are electrical impulses in this world. You will have no choice in the matter. A dog running up to you, a cat rubbing against you, a computer in the same room with you, even a mosquito landing for a bite, will make sure you live on and on and on. You will continue to exist without the luxury of technology or electronic toys in this modern world and without the touch of a loved one, much less another human being.

I believe this is more than an appropriate punishment for what you did to me. May you live forever with my name as a curse upon your lips.

*In love and hate,
Erin"*

Brad stared at the letter in horror, knowing that his life was forever changed. He had no idea if there was anything he could do about it. Apparently, he would have a very long time to think about the problem.

Following Advice

"**That hand cream** smells great. Where'd you get it?" Krista asked.

"The Body Shop. Unfortunately, they discontinued it. I got to buy the last of it on a great discount." Tracy removed the tags from the new work clothing she'd just bought.

"What shampoo do you use?"

"Just Pantene."

Krista nodded like she was mentally adding it to a list before asking her next question. "What about toothpaste?"

"Toothpaste? Why do you want to know that?"

"You have really nice smile. I like it."

Tracy shrugged. "Tom's of Maine, cinnamon-clove flavor. You're full of questions today."

"Oh, I know." Krista mimicked Tracy's shrug. "You have such a great life: new job, new apartment, great hair, you're really pretty, and everyone likes you. I guess I'm just trying to figure out your secret. What size do you wear?"

"Ten." She shook her head as she put the clothing away. "I don't have a secret. There's nothing special that I have or do. I'm just me. I figure out what I want, figure out how to get it, and I work my ass off for it."

"Is that it?" Krista watched her from a spot next to the bookshelf of Tracy's books and trophies.

"That it? Are you kidding? Do you have any idea what it took to find this place? I scoured Want Ads for days and drove all over the city looking for the perfect apartment. Things don't just fall into your lap, Krista. You have to work for them. You have to do the research and compare your wants versus your needs and make some hard choices."

"You know, you're right. I have been expecting things to come to me, but I do have to meet them halfway, don't I? I've been thinking about this for a while and that's what I'm going to do. I've figured out what I want and I'm going to do the work to take it. Starting right now."

Tracy hung up the last of her clothing. "That's really good. I can't wait to see what you come up with."

"You don't have to wait any longer."

She turned to ask what Krista meant, but the blow to her temple dropped her to the floor in an explosion of pain. Holding her head, she looked up and saw Krista standing over her. She had one of Tracy's trophies in her hand. Her 'Best Team Player' award she thought.

Krista hefted the trophy and swung at Tracy's head again. Tracy stopped it from hitting her in the head with her wrist. They both heard Tracy's wrist break. "No!" Tracy cried and tried to back away.

Krista spoke in a far too calm voice. "I decided what I wanted. I wanted to be more like you. I wanted your sense of style and determination. I even signed up with the same employment company as you. But, you've convinced me that I can't just want to be more like you. If I want to have the same life you have, I have to become more like you. I have to become you." She stepped forward, raising the heavy trophy again. "Thanks, Tracy. You really are the best. I'm gonna miss your advice."

Hell is Other People

MR. SMITH WAS a very important man. Mr. Smith was the CEO of a very important and prestigious communications company that did vital things with cable TV and the internet backbone. Currently, Mr. Smith was having the worst day of his life.

It all started with a last minute cross country trip to a partner company that threatened to pull out of a very lucrative partnership because of a hint that the government disapproved of their marketing strategy and future plans. Words like "monopoly" and "illegal" had been dropped in the partner's ear causing them to mention words like "contract" and "renegotiation."

The trip had been so last minute that Mr. Smith had to rush to the airport without his usual routine of setting up business meetings and evening activities. He was going to drop in on them... drop in like a ton of bricks from the way he was feeling.

The source of the current annoyance was two-fold: First, he had been forced to sit in Coach class in an aisle seat where he had been constantly bumped by passing people. Second, there was a baby screaming in his ear and had not stopped for more than a minute at a time the entire flight. Mr. Smith figured the little demon was sucking the souls out of the people around it during those brief moments of golden silence in order to have the energy to scream some more. It made concentrating on his work difficult.

Giving up on work for the moment, Mr. Smith decided to try and sleep. He closed his laptop and closed his eyes, wishing he were in the much more comfortable and civilized First Class. As soon as he fell asleep, something woke him. Something was touching his knee. He looked down and saw a dirty, peanut butter smeared child smearing more peanut butter on his pants as the child petted the soft fabric of his very expensive suit.

He snarled at the child to get away from him only to have a chorus of harpies pretending to be mothers descend upon him for scaring the now screaming child. The protests of "he's just a child," "he didn't know better," and "your suit can be cleaned" were drowned out by the original screaming baby in competition with the shrieking toddler.

It was at this time that the stewardess showed up to see what the "fuss" was all about. The result of the ensuing debate in which Mr. Smith had shown all of the decorum of being a Very Important Person despite the fact that he was dealing with lowly commoners was for the stewardess to go get a large man who spoke very sternly and condescendingly to him about the dangers of "air rage" and warned Mr. Smith that if he had another "outburst" he would be summarily arrested, handcuffed, and booked as soon as the plane landed. This would result in Mr. Smith being put on the "no fly" list for the rest of his life.

Mr. Smith, a very important man with a need to fly, calmed down, and fumed with the rage of an impotent man instead of the important man that he was. He forced himself to calm into a cold fury that he would use against his partner corporation if they didn't do exactly what he wanted them to do.

The rest of the trip was just as miserable. There was turbulence, more crying made worse by the comparison of the rare silences, and the battery in his laptop died, leaving him without anything to distract him from the hideousness of his situation. He swore to yell at his secretary for putting him in this position. Mistress or not, she needed to be punished for not finding him a First Class booking.

The landing felt more like they'd been shot out of the air than a controlled event and the warning that things may have shifted during the landing fell on deaf ears. As the plane came to a stop, people were already moving to open the overhead bins and a laptop case fell from above hitting Mr. Smith in the head. To add insult to injury, it was his own laptop case. It got stepped on several times before he could rescue it.

Things got worse still. Mr. Smith's seatbelt had gotten stuck and he was now trapped in his seat. After his row companions, impatient for him to move, clambered over him to get out, Mr. Smith hailed the stewardess by pressing the service light. While he waited for her finally arrive, he noticed a newspaper in the seat across from him. It had his picture on the front. Stuck in his seat, he couldn't reach it from his position. He craned his neck to read as much of the article as possible.

"CEO OF COMM CORP KILLED IN CAR ACCIDENT," the photo headline screamed at him. Disbelieving that a newspaper could make such a mistake of putting his photo in place of a dead man, he craned his neck more to read the caption below the photo. *"Tyler Smith, CEO of InternetPClink, Inc., was killed in a car accident today. He was on his way to the airport for a business trip with a partner company. InternetPClink, Inc. is about to undergo Federal investigation for unfair business practices."*

That was as far as he got when the stewardess arrived, carrying a clipboard. "Yes, sir?" she asked in her most polite 'fuck-you' voice.

"There's a problem here, Miss. My seatbelt is stuck. I need to get off this plane. I need you to fix this problem or cut me lose."

She looked at her clipboard. "No, Mr. Smith. You're fine. This isn't your stop. You'll be traveling on with us."

"No. This is my stop. I need to get off this plane," he said in his most reasonable shout.

She smiled again, venom dripping from the sweetness in her voice. "No, sir. You'll remain with us until you reach your final destination. Thank you for flying with Halifax Enterprise Locations Limited. You'll be flying with us for a long, long time." She turned around and picked up the newspaper. "If you will excuse me, I have other duties to attend to."

Ink

"**WELCOME TO THE** kick-off NaNoWriMo meeting of the Eastside Horror Writers Association." Chris bowed with a flourish to the other men and women around the table. "As you know, every November is the National Novel Writing Month where all of us, not just attempt, but complete the first draft of a new horror novel that we will review and edit over the next few months before submitting it to this group for peer evaluation. Of course, the minimum word count by NaNoWriMo rules is 50,000 words. But, here at the EHWA, we strive to make 60,000 words in the month of November. After all, we are *not* common writers. We're professionals and I expect us all to act that way."

Chris paused as the small group of authors applauded this last sentiment. "Thank you. Thank you. I know you all are anxious and eager to get started. However, we must wait until the clock turns twelve midnight to fill our fountain pens and get to work." He gestured to one of the waiting members standing off to the side. "Also, we need our traditional toast to the man who is going to make sure that all of our work over the next month will bear bountiful fruits based on our hard labor. Joseph, if you please..."

"I would indeed, Chairman." Joseph rose from his seat. "In past years, many an author has paid homage to wine in their great works. I felt it fitting for the EHWA to toast this year with Writer's Block Syrah 2005."

There was a smattering of light applause and some muted laughter at the name of this year's wine. "The Writer's Block Syrah begins with soft aromas of coffee, black berry, and tobacco. Flavors of plums, currents, and smoke are complimented within soft tannins that hint at chocolate. The finish shows a touch of anise, leaving a bit of spice upon its departure. It's a perfect beginning for our most productive month of the year."

"Thank you, Joseph. You've outdone yourself." Chris watched as Joseph poured the wine for everyone. When he was done with the membership, he brought a glass up to the Chairman who nodded his personal thanks.

"Now..." Chris watched the clock as the minutes and seconds ticked away. "...as is ritual and tradition for the Eastside Horror Writers Association, we begin every new NaNoWriMo novel with old fashioned fountain pen and paper. The ink we choose flavors our prose with its own qualities. I had to think carefully about the type of stories we wish to produce in the coming year. Should we focus on youthful independence and courage or old, jaded experience? Or perhaps something in-between?

"This year, I've decided that it's time to get down and dirty into the wickedness of the human soul and how it can be more horrific than the most terrifying demons we can dream up." He savored the anticipation. "This year's ink is made from the crassest, most unpleasant, and petty man in the county. I give you... Mr. McCreedy!"

With an elaborate gesture, Chris yanked the silken cord and opened the velvet curtains to reveal a middle-aged man bound tight to an old fashioned high back chair. He was conscious and aware, glaring at them as they applauded his appearance. Over his mouth was duct tape that hid a wad of fabric to make sure he didn't make too much noise. He began to struggle again when no one raised a voice of protest at his treatment.

"This toast is for you, Mr. McCreedy. May your sacrifice please our Patron and may your blood flow smoothly through our pens." Chris and the rest of the Eastside Horror Writers Association membership raised their wine glasses high before drinking it down in single effort.

"Come now, one and all." The Chairman beckoned. "It's almost time to fill our pens. Come everyone, step fully into the circle." He gestured to the large ritual circle around the chair that Mr. McCreedy sat in. "Make sure you fill your pens full and don't hit an artery. Some of us like to write our entire novel in ink."

The more the authors crowded around Mr. McCreedy with their sharpened fountain pens held high, the more he struggled in vain. This made the Chairman smile. Joseph leaned over to Chris. "I love the first night of NaNoWriMo. It always gets my heart pounding and my creative juices flowing."

"Me, too," Chris said with sincerity as he watched the grandfather clock at the far end of the room. Very soon it would be midnight and each of them would begin a new bestseller. Their Patron and their sacrifice would see to that.

A Special Breed

"**Hello James. Nice** to meet you." David let his new client in the door. He watched man with interest. Joe had recommended this person for a particular reason.

"Yeah. Nice to meet you. You the dog breeder?" James looked around the small apartment with some distain.

"I am."

"Great. I can't wait to meet the puppies. David told you what I was looking for in a dog, right? Aggressive, protective, obedient. Right?"

"Never fear, James. I raise a special breed of dog here. If there's a match, you'll never be without your dog." He led the client to the back room and opened the door. "We have six puppies in this litter. I recommend that you have a seat on the floor and wait for the puppies to come to you."

"It smells funny in here." James wrinkled his nose as he stepped into the room.

David shrugged. "It's the kind of smell you get when you keep a bunch of animals in an enclosed space. It's normal."

James sat down and watched the puppies come tumbling out of the double door closet. "Why are they in there?"

"These dogs are part wild. It's where their aggression and protectiveness comes from. That closet is what they consider to be their den." David leaned up against the wall next to the door and watched James with the puppies. After he scooped up the first puppy and lifted him, David reminded him, "It's best not to pounce on them. They might get upset. That wouldn't be good for the family."

"I want to see what kind of chops these guys have. They gotta be good and they gotta be fierce."

James turned the now unhappy puppy upside down.

"Dude. You don't want to do that. Put the puppy down." David straightened, looking alert. He kept an eye the closet door. "Seriously."

The puppy in James' hands started to yelp in a series of high pitched, unhappy yips that bordered on panic. The rest of the puppies turned towards James in a single motion and stared at him, their shoulders hunching and their fur bristling. James dropped the puppy down with a disgusted snort. "I thought you said these guys were aggressive. What a baby."

"Time to go." David opened the door. "You're outta here. I'm not selling to you. There's no way one of these guys would bond to you."

"No! David told me you were the best. I'm not leaving now." James reached out and grabbed a different puppy. It snarled in his hands. "That's what I'm talking about." The puppy turned and sunk his needle sharp baby teeth deep into the meaty part of his thumb. James cursed and dropped him. "Fucker bit me."

"Yeah. He did. He drew blood." David shrugged and stepped out of the door. He closed it behind himself and locked the door. While he engaged the deadbolts and put up the door brace, he heard the client moving and speaking. He opened the tiny one inch square peep hole in the door. "What was that?"

James stood and threw a kick at the circling puppies; all of whom were growling low in the backs of their throats. "Dude! What the fuck are you doing, locking me in here?"

"I told you it was time to go. Now, it's too late. They drew blood from you. That means you're prey." David licked his lips as he felt the puppies' mother prepare for the hunt.

James came to the door sucking his wounded hand. Before he could say anything, the growl of a very large creature made it to both of their ears from the depths of the large closet. "Holy shit... what was that?"

"That would be Mona." David smiled despite how much the sound of that growl frightened him.

"Let me outta here. You open this damn door now!"

"I tried to tell you. This was a very special breed of canine. Half canine to be precise. It's part wild. Their father was a German Shepherd. He didn't survive the breeding. But they did breed true. It was worth his sacrifice."

David stepped back as James slammed himself against the door. "I don't really know what Mona is. I do know she's bonded to me and that's the only reason I'm still alive. I love her. I really do. Right now I know she's hungry. It's feeding time... I promised her an occasional human meal. Looks like you're it and I owe Joe a puppy at half price. He said you'd be good pickings. He was right."

James' attention was no longer on David and getting out. It was on the creature named 'Mona' now that he could finally see her. "Jesus Christ! Oh, God! Help! Somebody help!"

David shut the tiny peephole, turned, leaned against the door, and closed his eyes as he said. "It's okay, good girl. You can have him. He's prey."

He listened to Mona go to work. James' screams were mercifully short as he felt Mona leap for the man, catch him by the throat, and slam him against the bedroom door. David could taste the prey's blood in his mouth and nodded. "Good girl, Mona. Go on. Your puppies gotta eat."

No Names

AMI LOOKED FOR more than casual fun at the dance club. She had one purpose, one goal. This was a good place to accomplish that.

As a lone woman, wedding ring or not, she was beckoned to the front of the waiting line. When she arrived there, after passing the gauntlet of leering men, the bouncer gestured to the first man in line. "This gentleman would like to pay for your cover if you would let him escort you in."

That was the way of things in this club. It encouraged more women to enjoy a night out and more men the opportunity to get into the exclusive club. It was why Ami always chose this club—a better class of men.

She looked at the man, handsome and well dressed, knowing that if she chose, she could pick a different man to 'escort' her into the popular club. However, he would do. She liked the color his eyes—green like hers. "I'm happily married. I'm not even going to tell you my name."

"Then I don't have to tell you mine." With a smile, he took care of her cover charge, handing over a twenty dollar bill to the bouncer then gestured for her to enter before him.

She liked that answer. It allowed her to fantasize about him at her whim—give him the name and attributes she wanted. He escorted her into the club and over to the bar, making a passageway for them both through the sea of bodies. He tilted his head in a wordless offer of a drink. Ami nodded her agreement.

He didn't tell her his name when he handed her the drink or as they danced the night away.

She didn't ask.

He didn't tell her his name while he worshiped her womanly curves as he helped her get very drunk.

She wouldn't ask.

He didn't tell her his name when he fended off the other predators or while he escorted her to the taxi... and then to the hotel.

She dare not ask.

He didn't tell her his name as they made hot, sweaty, anonymous love.

She didn't want to ask.

He didn't tell her his name when she stabbed him in the neck with her hidden dagger or as he drowned in her last kisses and died in her arms.

She couldn't ask.

Spell wrought and quickening done, her child would never know his father's true name and that was just the way she needed it to be. Her baby would have green eyes. Just like his.

Love Bites

LIZ WAS ALREADY in the bathroom putting make-up on by the time Gideon got up and stumbled towards the toilet. "You mind?"

"Nah." She smoothed liquid foundation across her check. "It's the hallmark of a good relationship when one can pee in front of the other."

He snorted in amusement and got to business. When he was done, he flushed the toilet and joined her at the double sink. First, to wash his hands. Second, to take stock of himself.

God, he looked like hell this morning. For that matter, he felt like it, too. He hoped he wasn't getting the cold that was racing around the office. He was always so good at fighting off bugs. Then, he noticed the bite marks and scratches all over his body. "Damn, girl, you did a number on me last night."

She paused in her careful application of foundation. "I didn't hear you complaining last night."

"Well, no. I was enjoying myself. But some of these marks aren't going to be easy to hide." He coughed and felt his head. He was hot. "Shit."

"What's wrong, baby?"

"I think I'm sick. I hope you don't get what I got."

"Already did, hon. I'm the one who gave it to you." She smiled in the mirror at him as she dug in her make-up bag for her eyeliner and mascara.

"Really? I don't remember you being sick."

"That's 'cause I was at work when I got infected."

His eyes widened. "Shit, Liz. You work at a genetics lab. Isn't that dangerous?"

"Yeah. But I survived it. Turns out that the virus worked better than anyone thought it would. Besides, I volunteered." She felt his forehead. "Oh, yeah. You got it good. Of course, it's going to get worse until you die. Then you'll feel much better. I promise."

He stared at her, looking for the joke. "W-what? Worse until I die? Liz, that isn't funny."

"I'm not joking, Gid. I infected you on purpose. It'll take about 24 hours for you to die. Then you'll be just like me." She smiled brightly at him in the mirror.

He coughed and pulled a towel around his shoulders, feeling cold even though he was sweating. "Like you how?"

"A zombie, silly!" She tweaked his nose and headed back to the bedroom where she took off her robe and he could see why she was applying her face make-up so carefully. The rest of her was a dead blue-grey-white color that skin should never be. At least, not on a living person.

She slid into a pair of pants. "I knew we were working on a zombie virus. Not that they called it that. They had some long name that meant living-dead parasite, but it amounted to the same thing. Except, unlike the movies, they wanted their zombies to be smart and to be soldiers. Of course, they also wanted them very compliant." She wriggled into a bra and her shirt, then turned to him, looking completely normal. "They can't always get what they want."

Gideon stared at her. "How could you have done this to me or to yourself?"

"I wanted it. You know I've always wanted something like this. Oh, there are the flesh cravings, but raw meat will suppress them for a while. Doc says we might get into live feeding with small mammals. He wants us to be careful with the human consumption. He wants to make sure it doesn't make us feral."

"You're serious. You're totally serious." He stumbled into the bedroom and collapsed to the bed.

Liz tucked him in. She petted his face while he shivered. "You poor baby. This is gonna be hard on you."

"Why me, Liz?"

"Well, we needed another test subject for the virus and it had to be male and I didn't want to go into this new world without you. So, I volunteered you." She stood and looked for her phone. "Besides, we all knew that you'd be one of the best zombie hunters out there and we just couldn't have that. Now, you'll be on our side, working with us instead of against us and we'll be together forever. Isn't that great?"

"As much as I love you, Liz, I don't want to be a zombie. I really don't. I don't know if I could control my urges. You know... all that flesh eating."

"Well, you're gonna find out because you have no choice in the matter. There's no cure for the zombie virus. No cure at all. I need to call this in and tell them I'm going to stay with you until you rise again." She gave him a hug and smoothed his hair back from his forehead. "Just think of it as an undead campaign but for real. A real life adventure with the possibility of living forever or at least hundreds of years. You're gonna be one of the Generals in this new world and I'm always going to be with you."

As bad as he felt, suddenly the prospect of becoming an intelligent, fast moving zombie didn't seem so bad. "Can I pick some people to take with us?"

"Of course, baby. We can have all the minions we want. Who's gonna stop us?"

Directions

"**ARE YOU SURE** this is it?" Kaylee asked.

Diana held up her paper. "Yeah. I'm sure. This is where Elspeth said to come. The directions say, 'Left on 45th until you reach the 'T' and then go left for about two miles. There will be a driveway on the right. Park to the side of the driveway and honk your horn. I will come get you.' That's what it says."

"Honk the horn again." The other girl said as she fussed with her makeup in the rearview mirror.

Diana did. It sounded very loud to both girls.

"I swear to God," Kaylee muttered, "this better be one killer of a party or I'm going to throttle her."

They waited about five minutes before Diana got out her phone. "Come on. Let's walk up the driveway. Maybe the music is too loud for them to hear us. I'll call her on the way up."

They got out of the car and started up the starlit dirt road they both assumed was a driveway. Diana opened her phone and called Elspeth. No answer. She left a message. "Hey Elspeth. It's Diana and Kaylee. We waited at the bottom of the driveway and honked the horn a couple of times. We figure you can't hear us so we're on our way up. We'll make our introductions there."

The two of them continued to walk along the dirt road for another five minutes though it seemed like hours. "Um, I don't know if we're in the right place. I can't see any lights on houses or anything."

Diana chewed her lip. "Let's go back to the car. I'll let Elspeth know." She pulled out her phone again and called. Again, no answer. "Hey Elspeth. It's Diana and Kaylee again. We're convinced that you lured us out here to kill us because this place is really scary. We're going back to the car. If we don't hear from you soon, we're gone."

"That was a little short."

"I know. But, I don't like this. Something seems wrong to me." Diana put her phone away.

"Well, maybe if you two actually followed the directions I gave you, you wouldn't be in this mess." Elspeth's voice floated from the darkness in front of them. It surprised both girls enough to make them jump.

"Dammit, Elspeth! We were..." Kaylee said, coming forward. Both she and her voice stopped when she got a good look at Elspeth. Diana bumped into Kaylee. Both girls stared.

Elspeth was in a gorgeous ball gown of sparkly black material and glittering jewels. She looked as if she was dressed more for a vampire ball than a frat party. In her right hand clashing with her archaic dress was a silver pistol.

"What the fuck?" Diana asked.

The rest of her words were swallowed by the sound of two gun shots and the cries torn from Kaylee and Diana's mouths. Both girls were on the ground and holding their right legs, writhing in pain.

"You shot us," Kaylee cried.

"I know. And, I suppose, Diana, you can now say, 'I told you so.' Because, yes, I did lure you out here to kill you. Not personally, mind you, and this isn't personal. It's just my turn to provide meat for the feast." Elspeth turned and handed the gun to an odd looking short man in a red hat who had appeared beside her. "I hate guns. So messy."

"You're gonna kill us?" Diana backed away from Elspeth and the small group of short, bumpy looking men in red hats who had gathered around the woman Diana had thought was her friend. Every movement jarred Diana's leg and sent waves of agony through her body.

"No. Not me. Them. Redcaps have a thing for human blood. But, if you had actually followed the directions and waited for me, I would have brought you to a frat house and given you a draught that would have made you sleep through the feast... and your deaths. As it is now, I've just kept you from being able to run away."

Elspeth waved a hand towards the girls. "Gather them up and take them to the feast room."

The hoard of Redcaps swarmed over to the girls, picking them up by whatever they could get their hands on. Kaylee and Diana screamed and struggled against the creatures in vain. The girls were momentarily silenced by the sudden appearance of the fey castle as the Redcaps dragged them across the moat bridge and inside.

An exquisitely dressed young man appeared at Elspeth side, "Friends of yours?"

She shook her head. "Not really. But, I wouldn't wish that on anyone. They'll keep those girls alive as long as possible while they're consumed whole."

"Such is the way of Redcaps." He offered her his arm.

"Indeed." Elspeth accepted the offer and the two of them walked across the moat bridge into the castle. All traces of what had just happened, and the castle itself, disappeared as Elspeth and her beau crossed the castle's entrance.

All that was left behind was an abandoned car, in the middle of a field, with directions to nowhere lying on the front seat.

We Don't Open Random Doors in this House

MARCUS LOOKED UP from his typing. It was quiet. Too quiet. With the innate sense of a parent and spouse, he knew something was wrong. Abandoning his work, Marcus hurried from his office to the garage. He found Melina there, staring at the floating door.

"Babe." He touched her arm. "Hon, come away from there."

Melina shook him off. "It just keeps appearing and disappearing."

"I know. It's why we can't park the car in here. Now, come on, get away from the door."

"But…"

"No buts, woman. We don't open randomly appearing doors in this house. I know you're white, but you've been living with me long enough to know that if a house yells at you to get out, you get out. If the dolls come alive, you incinerate them. If a mysterious package appears on the door, you mark it "return to sender" and, above all… when doors attached to nothing appear in the midair, you don't open them!"

She sighed and nodded. "Fine."

He herded her before him until he had the garage door locked and dead-bolted behind him.

Melina turned, "What do you mean "I know you're white but…""

Marcus glanced heavenward. He hadn't wanted to have this talk with her. Seemed he didn't have any other choice. "Right. You know how we asked all our friends what to do when the door started appearing?" He gestured for her to sit at the kitchen table as he got out the electric kettle, filled it with water, and turned it on.

"Yeah."

"Well, what'd they say?"

"Jim said yes..."

"White." Marcus put the kettle on the counter.

"Tonya said no."

"Black."

"Greg and Casey said... no and yes."

"Black and white."

Melina looked at him. "Are you telling me that every single one of our white friends said to open the door and every single one of our black ones said no?"

Marcus nodded. "Yes, ma'am." As Melina sat back, contemplating this, he put teabags into to two mugs, adding milk to both and sugar to his, he continued on with his train of thought. "It's because white people are more secure. Black people," he gestured to himself, "have had to fight everything because everything tries to kill us. White people are soft and dumb. Uh... not all of them, honey. Certainly not you." He added this last in a hurry at the storm clouds gathering in her furrowed brow.

"What does that have to do with any of this?" She glared as the kettle gave off a shrill whistle.

He turned the kettle off. "Well, I'm just saying, none of those popular horror movies would work with black people in the real world."

Melina shook her head. "None of those people knew they were in a horror movie."

Marcus gave her a look. "When the walls bleed, you know you're in a horror movie."

"Point." She eyed him. "But the door... it's just there. It could be an adventure."

"And what is the definition of an adventure?" He poured hot water into both mugs and brought them over to the table, settling the one without sugar in front of her.

Melina had the grace to look chagrinned. "A person a thousand miles away having a perfectly rotten time wishing they were anywhere else but there."

"You taught me that."

She pulled the mug to her and accepted the spoon he handed her. "I did."

"So..." Marcus sat across the table from her. "No opening randomly appearing doors, yes?" Her answer took longer than he wanted it to take, but was the one he wanted to hear.

"Yes. We leave the door alone." She paused. "But I really wish I knew why it chose this house to appear in. Don't you ever wonder...?"

He shook his head. "Nope. That way lies madness." In truth, he did wonder from time to time. Then his good sense return and he got back to work. "We good now?"

Melina nodded. "We good."

Marcus stood. "Right. Back to work for me." As he left the kitchen, he made a mental note to either put a silent alarm on the garage door or add a new lock. That damn floating door was far too enticing for anyone's good.

Five Minute Stories

Volume Five

Responsible

"OK, MISS..." the officer paused to look at notepad in his hand, "Roman. You've been read your rights. Do you understand them?"

The young woman at the table with her wrists in handcuffs gaze at him with resignation.

"Miss?" He paused again, looking at his notebook.

"Call me Cassie. Everyone does."

"All right. You can call me Brad or Officer Dean. Whichever you're more comfortable with. Do you understand your rights? Do you know why you're here?"

Cassie nodded. "Yes."

"Can you tell us why you were illegally giving flu shots to people?"

"What's today's date? And time?"

He frowned at the question. It was odd. He wondered if she was one of the crazy ones. They needed special care. "July 21st. 11:40 in the morning."

"Already? Time slips by so fast. It doesn't matter anymore, I guess. It's already started." Cassie sat up, looking older than her reported twenty-two years. "You want to know..."

She was interrupted by Officer Dean's partner, Jordan Maloy, coming into the room. He didn't look at her. Instead, he handed Brad a folder, opened, and pointed at something on the top page. The officer's frown deepened. "Miss..."

"Cassie."

"Cassie. This report shows that you weren't giving people flu shots. It's something the lab can't immediately identify."

"Yes. I know. It's what I was about to tell you." Her tone was one of infinite patience. Like she had done this before and knew what was going to happen.

The two officers looked at each other. Brad nodded. "All right. Tell me about it." The two men waited, focused on her, looking for signs of violence.

"It doesn't matter anymore. It's here now. It's started. I was giving out vaccines against what's about to happen. Has happened. The End Times are here. Armageddon. The Apocalypse. Whatever you want to call it. I wanted to save some people from what was coming. I didn't want to be the only one left alive. It'll move like wildfire through tall grass in summer. People will die in the streets with sores exploded all over their bodies. It is already moving—Seattle, San Francisco, DC, New York, Paris, Geneva, Saint Petersburg, Sydney... all over the world. People will die and no one will know how to stop it."

She gazed at the wall, seeing the horror in her mind. "Do you know how hard it is to choose who will live and who will die? To decide against your favorite nephew because he has a hereditary disease that requires constant medication and should not—cannot—be passed on to future generations? Do you know how difficult it is to choose strangers out of a crowd to become the saviors of mankind? You don't. But, maybe you will."

The two men looked at each other again, caught up in the reality of this woman's words. Finally, Brad shook his head. "I can't believe this, Cassie. I can't."

She shrugged. "Don't then. Send your partner out to check on the state of the world. If you don't trust me, trust him."

Brad motioned Jordan towards the door. Then, engaged in a silent staring contest with his prisoner. He was chilled to the bone to see no fear, no doubt, no hesitation on her face. Just weary resignation. She believed every word she said. She had to be insane. Had to be. The alternative was too awful to contemplate.

Jordan returned, his face pale. "All the lights are lit up. People are dying. Everywhere." He whirled on the woman. "What did you do?"

Brad put a hand on the man's shoulder, his eyes on Cassie. "'Everywhere' as in our town or 'everywhere' as in the world?"

"It's all over the news. Everywhere-everywhere."

"Why didn't you tell someone? Why didn't you warn us?" Brad's questions were directed at Cassie. "Why didn't you do something?"

"No one believes the apocalyptic vision. Most times, they blame the calamity on the prophet." Her eyes flicked from Brad to Jordan and back again. "Also, I *was* doing 'something.' I was saving some, but you two put a stop to it. I'm no longer responsible. You two are." She bared her teeth in the parody of a smile. "You confiscated the vaccine. There were ten doses left. No more than nine now. Probably less. They're yours. Yours to do with as you please. You get to choose who lives and who dies. You both are responsible for what little is left."

She stopped then, letting the sentence hang between them like a rattlesnake. It had bitten her more times than she could count and, finally, it was someone else's turn.

The Perfect Cut for the Perfect Match

"Damn, woman." Steve gasped from his supine, spread-eagled position on the bed, "That was fantastic." He laid his head back and gazed at the ceiling, finally seeing it in the light for the first time. Above him was an amazing mural where a fantastical scene played out.

Taylor leaned forward and kissed him. "It's the least I could do for my perfect raven boy." She got off him with a sigh to match his grunt.

He grinned. "You're vain about your work."

"I am. I'm an artist working on a masterpiece." She threw a robe on over her naked form. "The raven in flight has finally healed and cured."

He wriggled his arms to make the leather shackles jingle. "I suppose you have no use for me now. Or, are you going to keep me chained to your bed forever?"

"For the rest of your life."

"Is that how it is?" He relaxed into his bonds.

"I want to show you something. Something marvelous. It's as much for me as it is for my patron." Taylor tilted her head, "Do you want to see it?"

"Can I see it chained to a bed?"

"Yes. It's right in front of you." She motioned to a fabric covered wall.

"Okay."

She unveiled the wall-sized framed piece of art with a flourish and stood to the side, looking at it. Steve tilted his head up for a better look. To him, it looked like part of a finished product based on the sketched mural above him. "It's good but... it's got holes in it."

"I know." She said, stroking the smooth hide of stitched skin. Her fingers danced over the edges of the canvas where the hole in her sky would soon be filled. "It's not done, but soon this piece will be added. This is where your raven goes."

"My raven? The one on my back?"

"Yes." Taylor admired her growing masterpiece. Her hand slipped behind the framed edge of flesh and reappeared with a small, sharp knife. She turned to him with it visible in her hand.

It was only then that Steve realized the danger he was in. "Whoa! No. No... Taylor. No!" He struggled against his bonds, but they were too tight. It had been sexy and amusing when Taylor told him that she didn't want him to get away from her. Now, it was terrifying.

Hurrying to his side she shushed his struggles with murmured words. "Shhhh. No. It's fine, Steve. Everything's all right. I promise." As soon as he stilled, looking at her like a trapped wild animal, her knife was at his throat, slicing his carotid artery. She didn't move as she was sprayed with arterial blood. "Everything's just fine. No struggling. You can't bruise your back. No bruising my work. That's not allowed. You don't want to be memorialized by bruising my sky do you?"

"Taylor, God, Taylor... I don't want to die." His eyes pleaded with her.

"Oh, silly man. You aren't dying. You're going to live forever in my masterpiece. You're going to get to talk with all of the others sacrificed to make my work of art live." She leaned forward and kissed his brow with bloodied lips. "You'll see. You're not alone. Not now. Not ever."

Steve looked at the stitched mural of inked flesh and could have sworn he saw the grass waving in the wind, birds flapping their wings, and the water in the pond ripple. It all moved for a moment.

Then it was still again and her words brought his attention back to her.

"Everything will go dark soon. I cut you deep, but don't be afraid. When you wake up again, you'll be with me in a new place and will have plenty of time to meet your neighbors. I'm sure they're eager for new company."

Voicemail

YOU HAVE TWENTY-three voicemails.

Voicemail 1, left at 6:01pm: .... Click.

Voicemail 2, left at 6:03pm: .... "Dammit." Click.

Voicemail 3, left at 6:10pm: "Yeah, hi. This is Sam. I know we don't know each other, but I've been watching you for a long time and I thought that, you know, we could get together for coffee tonight, but you aren't answering your phone. So, maybe another night." Click.

Voicemail 4, left at 6:16pm: .... Click.

Voicemail 5, left at 6:20pm: "Yeah, hi. It's Sam again. I was wondering why you weren't answering your phone. I know you're home. I can see you in the window. I've seen you look at your phone. Are you just playing with me? I'm not sure I like this game. Pick up the phone, okay?"... Click.

Voicemail 6, left at 6:27pm: .... Click.

Voicemail 7, left at 6:30pm: .... Click.

Voicemail 8, left at 6:32pm: .... Click.

Voicemail 9, left at 6:36pm: .... Click.

Voicemail 10, left at 6:40pm: "Chris, it's me, Sam, again. Why aren't you picking up the phone? Don't you want to talk to me? I keep calling. It's only polite for you to answer the damned phone! Why won't you pick up the phone? I know you're there." .... Click.

Voicemail 11, left at 6:44pm: "Hey, Chris. It's Sam again. I'm sorry I yelled. It's just really frustrating. I've been watching you for so long and I finally got the courage to call you and now you're ignoring me and I don't know why. Why are you ignoring me?" …. Click.

Voicemail 12, left at 6:46pm: …. Click.

Voicemail 13, left at 6:55pm: …. Click.

Voicemail 14, left at 7:02pm: "What the fuck is this? Who the fuck is that at the door? A lover? Is that your fucking lover? How could you do this to me? After all I've done for you? After my confession of love to you? You betraying bitch. You cock-sucking, cunt-licking bitch. I can't believe you're doing this to me!" Click.

Voicemail 15, left at 7:03pm: "Pick up the phone, Chris!"…… Click.

Voicemail 16, left at 7:05pm: "Pick up the phone! Pick up the phone! Pick up the God damned phone or I'm gonna kill you. I swear I'll do it."…. Click.

Voicemail 17, left at 7:11pm: "Are you happy now, Chris? Are you fucking happy? I think I've broken my hand because of you. After everything I've done for you. You remember that guy who keyed your car? I made sure he never keyed anything ever again. What about that bitch who insulted you at the bar? She's never insulting anyone ever again. Ever again. And this is the thanks I get, you ungrateful bastard." …. Click.

Voicemail 18, left at 7:15pm: "Dammit, Chris! Do you want me to come up there and kill you? Is that what you want? Because I'll do it. Believe me, I'll fucking kill you and your lover. Rip both your fucking heads off. Stop kissing in the window. Stop it! Stop! Just fucking stop! I don't want to have to kill you, but I will if you make me!" .... Click.

Voicemail 19, left at 7:21pm: "Hey, Chris. Please, babe, pick up the phone. Let's work this out. Okay? Pick up the phone. Let's talk. I'm sorry I yelled before. Okay? Just pick up the phone. It'll all be okay. I promise." .... Click.

Voicemail 20, left at 7:24pm: "Pick up the phone, Chris. Pick up the fucking phone! I'm done being nice. I've tried to be nice. Pick up the phone. Pick. Up. The. Goddamned phone!" .... Click.

Voicemail 21, left at 7:26pm: ...... "What the fuck?" .... Click.

Voicemail 22, left at 7:28pm: ... "Damn it!" .... Click.

Voicemail 23, left at 7:35pm: "Hello. This is Sam. I just realized that I dialed the wrong number when I was calling my fiancée, Chris. After that, I just kept hitting redial. I didn't think I was calling the wrong number. I'm really sorry if I gave you a scare. This is just a little joke that my fiancée and I like to play with each other. Please disregard all of my previous messages. They weren't for you. It was just me having a little bit of fun. Sorry about that. Have a real nice day now. .... Click.

Two Letters

"**Hey, Mom...** this retirement party is for you, you know. Don't you think you ought to be out enjoying it?" Tonia stood in den doorway.

Paula looked up from her cluttered desk. "I know. I'm just finishing up a little paperwork."

"The work's never done, is it?"

"No, not usually. But this time, it almost is."

There was a silence then while Tonia watched her mother sign a piece of paper, fold it in thirds, and slide it into an envelope. Then, the older woman fumbled for her lighter. She didn't find it in any of her pockets.

Tonia stepped forward and offered hers. "Mom?"

Paula accepted the lighter and picked up a sealing wax candle.

"Can I ask you a question?"

"You just did." A hint of her mother's old devil-may-care smile made a brief appearance.

"You know what I mean." Tonia continued when her mother gestured for her to do so. "Why are you retiring? Government work's in your blood like business is in mine."

Paula stopped what she was doing. "Have a seat. I've got a story to tell you. Maybe you'll understand. Maybe you won't. But, I'm betting you will."

Tonia sat and watched the woman she'd always admired, but didn't always understand. How her mother could have stayed in government work while the business world had clamored for her skills and leadership, offering an obscene salary to boot, was beyond her. "I'm listening."

"You remember Terry Woodsworth?"

"Your predecessor. Sure."

"He sat me down on the night of his retirement party and said, "Paula, you've got to know that this is a job that will eat a man—or a woman—alive if they're not careful. The burnout rate is 100%. I know you're a good woman and right for this position. I also know that you're going to run into shit you can't handle. So, I'm giving you these." He handed me two letters. Both were sealed in wax. The first had the number one on it. The second had the number two on it.

"Then, he told me, "There will come a time when the shit will hit the fan and your world's gonna crumble. When that happens, open the first letter. It will tell you what to do. But it has got to be your very last resort, Paula. The very last." I agreed to this, thinking it was both strange and touching. Then he tapped the second letter. "When your world goes to shit again and there's absolutely nothing you can do to save it, open this second letter. But, like the first letter, it's got to be the very last resort. When you can think of nothing left to save the mission or your people, open this." Again, I agreed."

Tonia frowned, intrigued. "Did you ever open those letters?"

Her mother nodded. "Yes. I did. It's one of the reasons I've held this job as long as I did. Longer than any of the previous department heads."

"What did they say?"

"The first one was about a year into my stint as the Director. Really, everything was falling down around my ears. The mission had failed. My people were hurting. The sharks were circling. It was the point of no return. If I didn't do something, everything was lost. I'd tried everything and, for the first time, I realized that I really did need those letters. I opened that first one and was shocked."

"What did it say?" Tonia leaned forward. She was hooked. She had to know.

"It said, "*Blame everything on me. I'm long gone and couldn't care less what my rep is in the Department now. Do what you have to do.*" At first, I didn't want to, but immediately, a plan came to mind. So, I did. I did what Terry told me to do and it worked. I pulled our collective asses out of the fire at the expense of my old mentor's reputation." Paula flicked Tonia's lighter on and lit the end of the sealing wax. They watched in silence as the melted wax covered the first letter and Paula stamped her seal into it.

Tonia still hadn't found any appropriate words in response as her mother repeated the procedure with the second letter. This hadn't been what she'd expected. Finally, she asked, "Did you need to open the second one?"

Paula nodded. "Yeah. I did. A couple of weeks ago."

"And?"

She took a breath. "It said very simply, "*It's time for you to write two letters.*""

Waiting

JANE ARRIVED AT Biba's with her husband's anniversary gift in hand. They knew her here. This was their favorite restaurant. She and Tony had been coming here for years. Megan, their favorite waitress, took her to their favorite table. "A glass of the house Riesling while you wait?" she asked.

"Yes, please." It had been a wonderful day. Jane was so happy she'd found exactly the right thing for Tony this year. It was their fifty-second wedding anniversary. She placed the small package in red paper with white hearts on the table and slid it across to where Tony would sit when he arrived.

"What's this?" Megan asked when she returned with the wine.

"It's our anniversary. I found Tony the perfect gift." Jane smiled up at her.

"Oh! Can you tell me what it is? I won't tell anyone. I promise."

"Just because it's you. I found him a model car. It's a 1948 Fastback Cadillac. It looks just like his first car."

"That's wonderful! I'm sure he'll love it."

Jane nodded and smiled after the girl as she turned away to attend to other customers. She glanced at her watch and saw that it was five minutes past seven. She wasn't worried. Tony was always late. Something always caught his attention and when he realized the time, he would come running in, out of breath, and grinning that guilty little boy grin. She might scold him. She might not. She usually didn't unless he was really late.

As time passed and her first glass of wine emptied, she became more irritated. He wasn't usually this late. Especially on their anniversary. Megan refilled her wine glass with a few murmured words designed to soothe. But, they didn't. Tony should be here by now. He was going to get such a scolding for being late and for scaring her.

More time passed and she pulled out her cell phone. With shaky hands, she dialed his number and was ready to demand to know where he was until she heard the outgoing message. It startled her enough that she dropped her phone. Megan hurried over to get it for her.

"Is everything all right?"

Jane smiled a brave smile at her. "Yes. But, I think I need to be going."

Megan looked concerned. "Don't worry about the wine. It's on the house."

"Thank you, dear." Jane picked up her anniversary gift for Tony and shuffled out of the restaurant to her car at the end of the lot. By the time she reached it, the tears flowed freely down her face. She got in the car, but didn't turn it on. She hid her face in her hands and cried in great shaking sobs.

"Janie-dear. Don't cry." Tony leaned over from the passenger seat and put and arm around her. "Don't cry."

"I'm so sorry. I was so mad at you for being late. For keeping me waiting."

"It's all right now, sweetheart. I promise." He gestured to her lap. "Is that for me?"

She wiped at her face and nodded. "It is."

He took the gift and opened it up. "Oh, Janie! It's perfect. It's just like the car I had when we met."

"I know. That's why I got it for you. I was so happy when I saw it. I knew you would love it. I—" she looked at him, tears welling up. "I just forgot that you were gone."

"I'm not gone anymore. Everything's going to be all right now. I promise. Neither of us is waiting for the other anymore." He leaned forward and kissed her.

"You promise?" She searched his face.

"I do. Forever and ever." He tugged her hand. "Come on. I have my car over here."

Before she got out of her own car, Jane knew that she would be getting into the passenger seat of a dark blue 1948 Fastback Cadillac and was glad of it. "I love you, Tony."

"I love you, Jane."

"Forever and ever."

"Forever and ever." He smiled a loving smile and opened the Cadillac door for her.

*

When they found her the next morning, Mrs. Jane Shaw was resting peacefully in the driver's seat of her car with a smile on her face. On the seat next to her was an unwrapped package that had once contained a model car. The wrapping paper and bow were in the foot well of the passenger seat, but the toy car was missing. No one knew what had happened to it. It was never found.

A Gentleman's Protection

AS BILL AND Stephanie turned the corner onto the busy street, he shifted from her right side to her left side, putting him on the outside nearest the cars. He switched again back to her right side as they turned left onto a much smaller road. He paused, causing her to stop.

"What?"

"I can't decide if I should protect you from the cars or the blackberry bushes."

"Is that what you're doing with the switching sides thing?" She frowned at him.

Bill nodded. "Yep. A gentleman always walks on the outside to protect the lady from the cars. But, here... not a lot of cars, but a lot of thorny bushes."

She crossed her arms and started walking fast. "Well, I'm no lady so you don't have to be a gentleman."

He caught up with her, walking on the outside again. "Can't help it. I'm always a gentleman. It's how I was raised."

"How misogynistic."

"What?"

Stephanie stopped and turned on him. "Misogynistic. That's what I said. It's guys like you who keep trying to push women back into the kitchen. Let me tell you something, buster. We're strong. We're smart. We don't need your protection."

"Whoa. I didn't mean anything by it. It's just what my mom taught me." He raised his hands in a calming gesture.

She wasn't having it. She jabbed a finger at him. "Ever think that maybe I could do a better job of protecting you? I don't need or want your help."

By this time, Bill had stepped back from her. He was watching her and something behind her. "Are you so sure about that?"

Normally, Stephanie would have paused at the tone in his voice, but she was so filled with self-righteous anger that she ignored it. "I am. I don't need you to protect me."

He shrugged, his eyes cold and angry. "Okay."

Her victory smile was short lived. She cried out at the sudden pain in her arms. Blackberry bush vines actively twined themselves about her arms and tangled themselves in her hair. She fought against them as the thorns tore into her flesh. She yanked herself forward, trying to pull herself out of the writhing mass of flora that seemed to be trying to eat her. The bush's thorns ripped into her. It pulled her backwards towards its center. She wasn't strong enough to break free. Panicked, she grasped at Bill. "Help me!"

He smirked. "You want help after that big speech?"

"Yes!" She shrieked, being pulled backwards.

"All right. I'll help. I'll help the world get rid of horrible people like you who slap at politeness and manners, calling it a cage. The world doesn't need people like you." He reached down and grabbed one of her ankles, pulling it upward, putting her off balance.

Stephanie tumbled backwards into the thick blackberry bush and was immediately hidden from sight. He could see her struggles by the way the vines flexed and bent.

The bush became still. Bill stepped forward. "Well, now that you've had a good meal. I expect your berries to be extra sweet this year."

The blackberry bush shivered in agreement.

"All right. I'll see you guys later. Time for me to head back to work and mention that Stephanie detoured for a latte. I hadn't planned to give her to you, but she was being such a bitch. Just make sure you eat all of her within the next couple of days. Leave nothing behind."

One of the vines stretched out and stroked his cheek.

"You're welcome. You can always count on me. I'll always protect and feed you. It's just the way I was raised. Besides, you guys make the best blackberries I've ever tasted."

One Big Lie

"Liebig?" the waitress smiled. "That's a hell of a name to have grown up with."

Joseph Liebig nodded. "I know. I've been picked on all my life because of it. It's an Algonquian Indian name that just sounds like two English words put together."

"Really? What's it mean?"

He looked at her name tag. "Well, Ruth, it is hard to say in English, but it comes down to meaning 'animal-touched' and it seems to be true." He sipped his coffee.

She looked around the small roadside diner. It was off hours. They were practically the only people in the place. "Yeah? How so?"

He shrugged. "I breed dogs. Purebred golden retrievers. Some of them have won local dog shows, too. I just came from dropping off Goldy's brother."

"Goldy?" She refreshed his coffee.

"The last pup in this litter." He turned around and pointed at the truck parked in front of the diner. As if on cue, the small puppy that was watching through the window started yapping and jumping up and down. "Aww. She misses her brother. She likes company."

"Oh my gosh! She's so sweet. Can I see her?" Ruth didn't wait for an answer. "Bob! I'm on break!" At the grunt from the back, she smiled at Joseph. "Please?"

He grinned at her. "Of course. Do you have a house or a place where I can let her run around? We've been on the road for a while."

She was already taking off her apron. "Yeah. I have a place in back. It ain't much, but it's cheap."

Joseph got Goldy from the truck and followed Ruth around back. He hadn't realized the little shacks in back were homes, but apparently they were. He found they were nicer on the inside than outside. It was a good sized little home for people who didn't want much. He put Goldy on the floor.

"C'mere girl!" Ruth called and Goldy obliged by romping up to her, leaping into her arms, and covering her face with puppy kisses. Ruth squealed and laughed with delight. After about five minutes, she asked the question Joseph knew she would ask. "How much does a dog like this go for?"

"Goldy? She's not the pick of the litter, so only about $300."

Ruth's face fell. "Oh. That's a lot. I would love to have a dog like this." She sighed and pet Goldy who romped around her barking excited puppy barks.

"Would you now?" Joseph asked in a noncommittal voice.

"I would." Ruth paused. "I don't have $300, but I have something you might... might want?"

Joseph shrugged and watched her run to the only other room and dig through a box. She came back to him with a small black velvet box and offered it to him. He took it and opened it up. There was a diamond ring in it. A real one.

"I was going to keep it for my own wedding, but I don't have any prospects. I'd rather have the dog. I'm sure the ring is worth $300. Maybe $400. It was my grandmother's."

"You'd give up your grandmother's engagement ring for Goldy?"

"I would." She looked down at the puppy with pure love in her eyes. "I really would."

Joseph shrugged. "I can't take this ring, but you can have the puppy. You'll love her until the day you die. I can't ask for more than that. I really can't." He put the box down on the table.

"You mean it? You really mean it?"

"I do."

She threw her arms around his neck and hugged him while Goldy jumped up and down beside them. "I'm buying you lunch!"

"Nah, it's okay. I'll buy my own. You stay here and I'll go eat something. You're on break anyway." He patted her arm. "You play with the puppy... *your* puppy... and I'll see you when you get back on shift."

Joseph made his way back into the diner. The cook nodded at him with a particular smirk. From that look, it seemed that Ruth did more than just take breaks in her little home. "Coffee?"

The cook got it for him and left him alone with his thoughts. He contemplated the conversation about his name. It was amazing what people would believe. He made his name "Liebig" because that's exactly what he was. One big lie. And yet, they fell for the story every single time. No one was willing to call him on it when he used the word "Algonquian."

After about ten minutes, he put a fiver on the counter and walked out around back to Ruth's house. Without knocking, he opened the door and walked in. A tall Indian woman stood up from her meal. She wiped the last of Ruth's blood off her face.

"You happy?" He asked.

She nodded. "Sated for now." She walked over Ruth's half eaten body to the table with the ring box. "Is this real?"

"Yeah. Worth a lot more than $300 or $400."

"Well, she doesn't need it anymore." She handed it over to Joseph and transformed back into the golden retriever puppy.

He bent over and picked her up. "She doesn't need you or anything else anymore." He walked out with the ring in his pocket and the Wendigo in his arms. It would be hours, maybe days before people went looking for Ruth. By that time, both of them would be long gone.

Within the Lines

"I LOVE YOU, my darling Patricia!" John said.

"love you, too. But what about your wife?" Patricia threw herself into her darling's arms and hugged him tight.

"I hate her. I don't know what to do about her. She won't leave me alone. She's never going to leave us alone."

"There's only one thing to do, my only love..." Patricia paused dramatically, "We must kill her!"

John gasped, "You would do that? You would kill her for me?"

"Of course I would. I would do anything for you. Besides, I hate her, too."

He nodded. "Then, we must do it when she comes home tonight."

"Yes. I know just how to do it, too." Patricia walked into the kitchen and pulled out the biggest, sharpest knife from the drawer. "We'll stab her to death!"

John came over to the kitchen and picked up the next biggest, sharpest knife from the drawer. "You're so smart, Patricia. That's why I love you so much. We'll stand behind the door and stab her once she comes in."

"I love you, too, John-dear. That's a great idea." Patricia said.

So, the two people who really loved each other more than anyone else in the whole world waited in the entry hallway for John's wife to come home from work. She worked late a lot, always making dinner late, and being grumpy after working such a long day. Well, today was going to be the last day she would be late and the last time she would yell at John or Patricia because she had a bad day.

When John's wife came through the door, both John and Patricia stabbed her over and over and over again. They stabbed her so much that her white dress turned red and splattered blood all over the place. She looked at Patricia with blood dripping all around and said...

*

"Patty, honey, what are you doing?"

"Just drawing, mommy. Telling myself a story." Patricia looked up from the kitchen table. "Wanna see?"

"In a moment. It's been a long day and I'm tired."

"Whatcha got there, Squirt?" John, mommy's new husband, craned his neck as he took his coat off.

"A drawing. Wanna see?" Patricia turned to him with hopeful eyes.

"Of course I do." He came over to see. "That's very good! It's that you?" He pointed to a smaller figure.

"Yes. And that's you." She pointed to the John figure.

"That was my next guess. What's in our hands?"

Patricia lied. "Microphones. We're singing to Mommy."

"Mommy's the one in the red dress?" He looked up. "Hey, Sharon. You've got to see this. Your daughter is really talented. She drew all of us."

Sharon came over and looked at the drawing as John pointed out Patricia and himself singing to her on Patricia's drawing. Sharon smiled in a distracted manner. "That's very good, honey, but you need to learn to keep your colors within the lines."

"Okay, Mommy." Patricia's smile disappeared as her mother headed down the hallway.

John noticed and gave her a kiss on the forehead. "Don't worry about it, Patricia. I love it. You're very talented."

"Thanks, John." Patricia smiled brightly knowing that her daydream of Mommy's death and her own marriage to John will happen one day very soon.

The End.

Origin Story?

I REMEMBER SOMEONE once said that being a telepath was like living in a hotel with very thin walls. You could always hear the movements and mutterings of the people next door to you and, if you concentrated, you could make out what they were saying or doing. But, you could never, ever completely shut it out.

I used to think that whoever said that was either an author trying to portray an angsty person or someone who was just a wet blanket and no fun to be around anyway.

I always thought that being able to hear the private thoughts of others would be so interesting and provocative. You know, with all of the stats about how men think about sex every seven seconds and women think about it every thirty-two seconds.

I would go to hotels just so I could listen to the voices through the walls. Just so I could feel like I was telepathic... Special. Blessed. I would spend days there. Sometimes, I would forget that I was listening with my ears and not my mind. Those moments were special, priceless even.

But you had put a stop to that, didn't you? You ruined my wish to become a telepath. I have the potential. I know it. But after my experience with you, I hope to God it never happens. You ruined my perfect dream the day you moved into the apartment next door.

'Shut up you stupid bitch!'
'You want me dead, don't you? I should kill myself right now and then where will you be?'
'Can't you do anything right?'
'Who will take care of you if I leave you? No one. That's who.'
'I wish I was dead!'

Over and over and over. I listened to your rants, your curses, your threats, and your violence. I had no way of turning it off. You would wake me up with your shouts. I thought I would go crazy. It was then that I realized that your constant invasion into my life on a daily basis is what it would be like to listen to people's thoughts; to be telepathic. It wouldn't be like turning on and off a radio at my whim. It would be hell.

I will never forgive you for that.

I've learned to hate you over the last few months and when I say "hate" I really mean it. I'm going to use that hate to kill you. Murder you in cold blood and there's no way anyone will be able to trace to me.

I've been cursed with something called pyrokinesis. I can't always control it. I killed my family accidentally. I destroyed the beach house and burnt down part of the school gym. I've hated myself for this curse for so long.

But, because of you, I've been practicing in my apartment fireplace. I've been practicing for about a month. Because of you, I've been exercising this hateful power. I've been using it despite *everything* I promised myself years ago.

You know what I've discovered? I like it. I like to burn.

Now it's your turn.

The New Line

"**Here's the two** shirts, two pairs of pants, and the skirt you asked for." Jane handed over the clothing through the dressing room door. She noted that the customer was racking up an impressive number of clothes and a bunch of it was on the floor. She kept her professional "the customer is right" face on the surface while she sighed inside. It was getting late and she couldn't go home until all of the dressing rooms were clean.

Amber thanked the salesclerk and hung up the clothing on the different hooks. She had seen the look the salesclerk had given the messy dressing room and felt guilty. She would make sure to re-hang everything before she left. It was just that she was having a really bad clothes day. Even her favorite boutique was failing her and that was really upsetting her.

Standing in her bra and panties, she chose a sweater to go with the skirt she had to get in a different size. Both larger than normal and that didn't do a thing for her ego except stomp it into the ground. The skirt slid on and fit perfectly. It was the first time all evening something fit right. It made her smile, even if it was a size bigger than it should have been.

After posing for the mirror, pleased with what she saw, Amber took the sweater and wriggled it over her head, betting it would look smashing with the skirt. However, the neck of the sweater got stuck on the bridge of her nose and would not move any further. Amber flailed, stuck in the sweater at an awkward angle, caught up in the clothing. After a massive amount of wiggling and gyrating that would've made a sailor blush, she managed to get it off again.

In disgust, she threw the sweater to the ground where she had thrown a number of her rejects, and decided to cut her losses, just buy the skirt and go. She eyed the mound of clothing, mentally debating whether or not she should stop to hang it all up again. Then she saw the sweater move and jumped back.

After a few moments of stillness, Amber prodded the pile of clothing with her foot. The entire pile exploded, whirling around her in the dressing room. Amber turned to flee from the incomprehensible situation, but a t-shirt she had discarded wrapped itself around her hand, binding it shut. She tried with her other hand, but a pair of jeans lassoed it and pulled it away from the doorknob and freedom.

Amber stumbled backwards, not able to see in the flurry of flying clothing. The skirt, that had fit so perfectly before, was now cinched tight around her body, hampering her movement. She couldn't breathe.

Amber managed a single, muffled cry for help before a sweater slammed itself into her face, wrapping it arms about her neck and constricting tight. She fell over as the rest of the discarded clothing in the dressing room covered her from head to toe in a cocoon of clothing—impossibly alive and hungry.

Out in the shop, Jane hurried towards Claire who was locking up for the night. "Wait. We still have a customer in the shop."

Claire shook her head. "No we don't." She continued to lock the door and turn the sign to show that the shop was closed. She flipped off the front lights.

"Yes, we do. I just gave her more stuff to try on." Jane looked back over her shoulder towards the dressing room. "She's got quite the pile of clothing in there, too. I hope she's going to actually buy some of it."

"Trust me on this. There's no customer back there." Claire was serene and confident.

Jane opened her mouth to protest again, but then they both heard Amber's single cry for help. Her eyes opened wide. "Oh, hell. Is it that time again?" The other girl nodded. "I completely forgot."

"I didn't." Claire watch the room with cautious fascination. All of the clothing in the store moved. Small motions, like a breeze through tall grass. "Especially when I saw you getting her more of the same stuff in different sizes. You know our clothing always fits. Always."

The two of them walked carefully through the racks of clothing. Claire didn't shrink away from the caressing touches of sleeves as Jane did. Claire sighed impatiently. "I told you, you're family. You work here. They'd never hurt you. Besides, they've chosen their sacrifice. It was Amber. They only take one a season."

Jane straightened and endured the touches. It still unnerved her to see the clothing come alive. Most of the time, she tried not to think about it. "Yeah. It's too bad. She was a good customer. Even if she was making a big mess back there."

Claire shrugged. "More will come. They always do. Besides, you know what this means, don't you?"

"Oh!" Jane gestured to the store. "The new clothing line! I can't wait to see it."

Claire touched one of the clothing racks with an affectionate pet. "Me neither. So, we'd better get out of here and leave them to their meal and their transformation. We'll see the new line in the morning."

"Yep. I'll have my 15% employee discount card ready. We sell the best clothing."

"At some of the cheapest prices." Claire paused then added. "For most people. For some, they cost everything."

Cassandra's Little Brother

"**Fabulous up-sell** on the Parker file, Leo!" Carl tapped his desk with a boney finger.

Yeah. Fabulous now. By this time next month, he'll be cursing my name. I smiled at him anyway. "Thanks, boss. That's just a little sugar to sweeten the medicine I'm about to give you." Sweetened with poison. No more than this bastard deserves.

"Yeah? What medicine is that?"

I held out the letter to him. "I'm resigning."

"Shit! Leo, no. Why? You're my best agent." He took the paper with a frown, reading it, and rubbed his thinning hair with the other hand. "Dammit."

"I don't want to, but I got to. My mom's real sick and I need to go take care of her until... you know." The lie falls from my lips like a well-loved gem of wisdom. This isn't the first time I've said it. In fact, it's closer to the thirtieth. And it won't be the last.

"Damn. That's rough." Carl shrugged. "Well, you do what you gotta do. If you get back this way, you've always got a job with me." He offered me a thin hand.

I shook it, knowing that the shit would hit the fan starting next month with the Parkers when Mr. Parker is murdered and their 'wrongful death' insurance kicks in.

By this time next year, this place'll be struggling with bankruptcy and in two years it'll be nothing more than a bad memory. Somewhere along the line, Carl will realize that every legitimate insurance claim had me as an agent and that, somehow, I up-sold every client the exact right insurance that they needed.

Somehow indeed. It's child play when you can see the shit coming. I'm a pre-cog, but no one believes an oracle when it's bad news. Unless they're an insurance agent.

At first, I tried to stop what I saw. The insurance gig was a happy coincidence. My first client walked in and I saw him killed by a drunk driver. I showed up at the spot to save him and it turns out I was part of the plan. I tried to warn him. He didn't believe me. I talked to him just long enough for the DUI to round the corner and come barreling down on him. His blood splattered all over me. I can still feel his blood hitting my face.

The next client I saw disaster for was an arson case. I had learned my lesson with the victim of the DUI. I didn't do something as stupid as to try to stop the arson. Instead, I sold Mr. Tyler as much fire insurance as I could shove down his throat. I got a nice bonus from that up-sell. Six months later, Mr. Tyler shook my hand and thanked me for being so insistent on the fire insurance.

By that time, I had become stupid drunk on this new way of helping the people. Stupid happy and stupid blind.

It wasn't until a year later when my boss, Frank, called me into his office and questioned my client list that I realized I'd made a mistake. Every claim that had come in had my name on it. Every single one was paying out more than the norm because of my up-sells. I begged off, claiming ignorance. How was I to know when bad stuff was happening?

How indeed? Frank badgered me for an hour. He wanted to know how I knew and he wanted to know why I up-sold instead of denying them insurance as a bad risk—which they clearly all were in retrospect.

In short, Frank wanted to know why I hadn't been a bastard like him. I maintained my innocence through it all. In the end, he fired me and said he would just cancel everyone's insurance when the time came instead of renewing it.

I got the last laugh. Everyone whose claim was going to come in from that group came in before their term was up. The rest were solid, safe sheep and he cut off the revenue when he needed it most.

But I learned a very valuable lesson from Frank. I can't stay more than a year with any one company. So, I find the sleaziest, most hateful bastard I can find to work for, impress him with my up-sell numbers, and get hired on. Then, when the year's up, I trot out that tried and true lie about a sick mom and I'm gone before all the claims start coming in.

The running gets old quick. I've been doing it for a long time. Eventually, they'll catch up to me. It's only a matter of time. I'm not running from them. I'm already caught, but that won't happen for years. I think. Instead, I'm running from the people I've helped along the way. I can't bear to look at their grateful faces knowing what's coming next. I can't tell them and take away that hope. Hope is too damn important.

I know this on a personal level. Just like I know, eventually, I'm gonna be caught. By whom? I don't know. When? I don't know exactly. Where? I suppose I'll recognize it when I see it. But I have hope because after that point in time, I can't see any more.

I know I'm not dead. I just know I don't know what's coming next and you have no idea how much that terrifies and relieves me. I have the hope that when they catch me, they'll be able to take away my curse and I'll finally be able to live like a real person.

I've got to have that hope. It's all I have left.

Legacy

"**KNOWING YOU, YOU** don't want to touch that." Monte continued to straighten up his rare bookroom in the back of his store.

Elli withdrew her hand from a glass case where she'd been reaching for an odd looking book. It seemed delicate, stiff, and had wrinkled edges. The book's binding was colored in a subdued yellow, with sporadic brown and black splotches, like an old banana. "Why? Is it cursed?"

"Of course."

"Nuh-uh." She glanced at it. "Cursed how?"

He rolled his eyes. "No. It's not cursed, but it always creeps people out."

"Why?"

"Because it is bound in human skin."

"Nuh-uh." She glanced at it again. "Really?"

Monte nodded. "Really."

"Dude, isn't that, you know... illegal?" Elli reached touched the book with a gentle fingertip. It didn't feel any different than any other book bound in leather.

"No, 'dude.' It isn't." He gestured to the book that Elli stroked. "It is a practice known as *anthropodermic bibliopegy.* It was sometimes used in the 18th and 19th centuries when accounts of murder trials were bound in the killer's skin."

"Weird." She picked it up and flipped through the pages. "It's in another language. What's this one about?"

"It's in French. It's about one of my ancestors, his murder trial, and his execution."

"Nuh-uh." Elli tilted her head. "You have a murderer in the family?"

Monte nodded. "Yep. He wasn't the only one either. I have a couple more of this type of book. All but one was put to death for murder."

"And the one that wasn't?"

"She was a cadaver. She willed her body to science. To honor her for this, they made a book of anatomy bound in her skin based on what they discovered from her body. It's in English and Latin."

"You know, this is both kinda creepy and kinda cool."

"Cool?" Monte stopped his cleaning to look at her. "You think *anthropodermic bibliopegy* is cool?"

"Well, it's stranger than fiction and more interesting because it is real. Plus, in a way, these people get to spend the rest of their... existences... so to speak... with books as a book. Books are awesome." She continued to look through the human-hide bound book. "It's not such a bad way to go. It leaves a legacy. I like that. And I like books."

"I'll remember that when I decide to murder you."

Elli looked up. "But you wouldn't, would you?"

He shrugged. "Murder seems to run in the family. Never know when I'll snap. Just consider yourself fair warned. If I ever come at you with this," he reached behind the counter and pulled out a hefty looking claw hammer, "you know you need to run." Monte bounced the head of the hammer against his palm.

She stared at him without moving. "Nuh-uh," She said without conviction.

Monte barked laughter. "You believe me!"

Elli put the book down. "No. I didn't. You're just being weird. You wouldn't hurt me." She gathered up her things. "I have to go and it's not because I think you'd make a book out of me. I just have to go. You wouldn't hurt me."

He nodded without comment and watched her go. Some people were so gullible. It was one of the reasons he liked Elli. He wouldn't hurt her. Not yet in any case. She was right about that. Not while her story was still incomplete.

Monte walked over to the table where Elli set the antique book. He picked it up and smiled at it. "All things in due time, eh, Gramps? Isn't that what you always said? If a project was worth doing, it was worth doing well." He reverently set the book on its stand behind the protective glass doors.

"Yes..." The word was a whisper of fetid breath on the back of his neck.

Living up to his Great-Great-Grandfather's legacy wasn't an easy task—especially with his hungry spirit always watching—but it was one he was determined to do and to do well.

Elevator of the Damned

NICK STOOD WITHIN the silent group of people in the elevator. There were four other people, forcing him to stand in the middle of them. He was already unhappy. No one liked to go to the dentist. Especially not for surgery. His stomach roiled at the thought of his gums being cut open and his teeth pulled. The more he thought about it, the more he wanted to hide in one of the corners already occupied.

The elevator stopped on the ninth floor and the doors slid open in a hurky-jerky manner that didn't inspire confidence. A man stood there. He made no move to get on the elevator. He looked Nick in the eye and said, "Don't you know you're all damned?"

As the elevator doors shut, they looked at each other. Nick gave an uncomfortable chuckle. No one said anything as the elevator stopped and he got off, still thinking about the man. He'd been familiar. Nick didn't know why. He didn't think he'd seen the man before. Shaking his head, Nick forgot him and headed to his next appointment.

*

The elevator was crowded, but Nick pushed his way onto it anyway. He was almost late as it was. Hemmed in by people on all sides, he'd never felt more alone. This was it. One window for marriage licenses. One window for divorces. Not that he'd wanted his marriage to end. The thought of losing his wife was a stab to the heart. His stomach twisted and turned, threatening to expel what little he'd eaten.

The elevator stopped on the ninth floor. A familiar man stood there. He looked at the crowd. Instead of saying he'd take the next elevator, he said, "Don't you know you're all damned?"

No one said a word as the elevator doors shut. Nick scowled, anger pushed away his loneliness and regret at the end of his marriage. Who the hell was that guy to say something like that. He forced his way to front of the elevator as it stopped on his floor. Divorced, maybe. Not damned. He stomped away, pushing the thought of the man from his mind. He was already late.

*

The elevator was empty and cold. Nick stepped within. It was as if he were already standing in a morgue next to his child. He hugged himself, fighting to keep the tears off his face. He failed. Tears streamed down his cheeks. He was helpless to stop them. Just like he was helpless to do anything to make things better for his child.

The elevator stopped on the ninth floor and opened. A single man stood there and gazed at Nick in his tear stained glory. He made no attempted to get on the elevator. Instead, he looked Nick in the eye and said, "Don't you know, you're damned?"

The elevator doors slid almost shut. Rage moved Nick. Before he understood what he was doing, his hand shot out and he halted the elevator doors. With a strength he didn't know he had, he forced them opened again and stepped out into the hallway. "How dare you?"

"No," the man said. "Not I. How dare you?" He smiled now.

Nick blinked at him, shocked. Lifetime after lifetime cascaded over him. He shook his head. "I've never been in a car accident. I've never watched my father shoot himself. I've never been married. I've never had a root canal. I don't have children. What's happening? This isn't my life... I didn't do these things." He hunkered down in the hallway with his hands over his head.

The man hunkered next to him. "No, but you've experienced it all. Ever terrible thing that anyone has ever thought about in an elevator." His voice was gentle.

"Why? Why is this happening?"

"Because you believed it needed to happen. And now, you believe, somewhere deep inside, you've been punished enough."

Nick shook his head. "I don't understand."

The man helped him up. "I know. You will. Now that you're ready to let yourself understand... and move on... you will."

Nick let himself be shepherded down a long corridor of no color and every color. "Am I dead?"

"Yes. But that's all right. There's so much more to come."

"What was... what was the elevator?"

"The hell of your own making. You made it. You designed it. You suffered in it. We are always hardest on ourselves."

Nick knew the truth of the words, but not why he'd done it. "Who are you?"

"The one who's been waiting for you. It's time to move on. There's so much more for you to see."

"Is it good?"

"I think so."

With a lightness he hadn't felt in an eon, Nick nodded. "Okay. Let's go. I'm ready."

And he was.

Message from Jennifer Brozek and Apocalypse Ink Productions.

If you received this book without paying for it or having it gifted to you, please consider going to Apocalypse Ink Productions (www.apocalypse-ink.com) or Amazon.com to purchase another book from either Jennifer Brozek or the publisher. Apocalypse Ink Productions is a small press and we really do try to do right by our authors.

Thank you.

About the Author

Jennifer Brozek is a Hugo Award finalist and a multiple Bram Stoker Award finalist. Winner of the Australian Shadows Award for best edited publication, Jennifer has edited fifteen anthologies with more on the way, including the acclaimed *Chicks Dig Gaming* and *Shattered Shields* anthologies. Author of *Apocalypse Girl Dreaming*, *Industry Talk*, the *Karen Wilson Chronicles*, and the acclaimed *Melissa Allen* series, she has more than sixty-five published short stories, and is the Creative Director of Apocalypse Ink Productions.

Jennifer is a freelance author for numerous RPG companies. Winner of the Scribe, Origins, and ENnie awards, her contributions to RPG sourcebooks include *Dragonlance*, *Colonial Gothic*, *Shadowrun*, *Serenity*, *Savage Worlds*, and *White Wolf SAS*. Jennifer is the author of the award winning YA *Battletech* novel, *The Nellus Academy Incident*, and *Shadowrun* novella, *Doc Wagon 19*. She has also written for the AAA MMO *Aion* and the award winning videogame, *Shadowrun Returns*.

When she is not writing her heart out, she is gallivanting around the Pacific Northwest in its wonderfully mercurial weather. Jennifer is a Director-at-Large of SFWA, and an active member of HWA and IAMTW. Read more about her at her blog or follow her on Twitter at @JenniferBrozek

Apocalypse Ink Productions is an independent press focused on dark speculative fiction and horror in its fiction line and online based writing education in its non-fiction line.

Please visit our website at http://www.apocalypse-ink.com to learn more about us, and to find information on other books—both digital and print—that we have available.

CPSIA information can be obtained
at www.ICGtesting.com
Printed in the USA
FFOW02n0256110518
46507130-48472FF